Kissing Wounds

Paula Klim

Contents

Chapter One

In the early hours of the chilly fall night, my family, the Parks, were already having dinner in our small dining area. The noise of plates being pushed around, and my youngest sister occasionally whining when she didn't have her way made the place undoubtedly homely. The room was dimly lit, and we were having mashed potatoes with kale and Boursin cheese. The house cat moved about in the background, purring when it settled down on a counter in the kitchenette across from the six-person dining table.

I was sitting on the edge, smiling as my father gave me an earful about the two-year mission I was about to embark on. I would be the first-ever to go in my family since my parents had been converts and hadn't had the opportunity to go when they were younger.

"Now, stop it. I'm sure he understands." I heard my mother say as I felt her small hand place itself on my shoulder, I looked to my side, catching her small smile. Her hair was done in a bob-cut, and her other hand was preoccupied with holding a metal tray. My two other siblings were on the table too. Jessica who was twelve ate her food quietly, and Catherine who was five played with her food as she hummed one of the rhythms her teacher taught them in class off-key.

We all had our signature black straight hair, and skin that was a little bit tanned. My siblings and I looked like a good mix of my father and mother, we all got our mothers height and overall stature — which was not very good for me since I was a bit short for my age — 5'4, and we all got my father's face if that makes sense. Thin lips, small noses, and long well-defined faces.

"Honestly, I'm kind of sad to see you go," my mother said as she let go of my shoulder and made to drop the tray of food at the center of the table before pulling out the seat beside my father and sitting down. "I'm worried as well. It's not just your father."

"You know you're the first person doing this in our family, so we're right-fully worried," my father said, repeating what he had been telling me since the beginning of dinner. He was middle-aged, and his hair was already going white. he and my mother had started having children a bit later than most couples around town.

I rolled my eyes, resting back on my seat. "I'm going to another town while some people are heading over to different countries. Come on, I'll be fine," I said, looking at both my parents before giving them a small smile. They had suggested I wait a little longer. I was currently eighteen. I had just graduated like most of my peers. Sure, some people did their missions later in life, but I didn't think I wanted to be that random person in their twenties walking around with a majority of teenagers.

"And," I started, watching my parents, "Olivia's coming along with me. She's at my station. I'll be fine," I said, and I watched my other sister's eyes move to her plate as she sat down beside my father. Olivia and her family were long-term friends of ours. She was a red-haired nice girl. If I wanted to do anything I just mentioned Olivia and my parents let me. She was like my get out of jail card sometimes.

"I know you two are worried but trust me, things will be alright," I said, and my parents didn't say anything in reply, instead they returned their gaze to their food and continued eating. After dinner, I excused myself and headed upstairs to my room. I immediately went ahead to look through my boxes again, occasionally stopping to check my phone. Most of my mates were talking about it — talking about their missions and how excited they were to go.

I was excited to go too. I was very excited. During the last year of high school, I had fallen back on my relationship with God. I just sort of floating around and concentrated on school work until my church started asking last year students if they were going to take part in a mission. That had given me something to look forward to, and now, after some light training, I was ready to go spread the word with some of my friends at my side.

Just as you learn more by teaching or tutoring someone I was bound to learn more by preaching to people, right?

I didn't have much time to think about my theory since my phone went off in my pocket. I fished it out, unlocking the screen before tapping the notification I had gotten from Olivia.

Message from: Olivia.

Hey! How are you? Are you excited? We have three more days until we leave.

THURS, 8:07 PM.

Excited? I'm overwhelmed! I thought to myself but just smiled before typing up a reply to her.

Message to: Oliva.

I'm excited.

I can't wait to spread the word!

THURS, 8:08 PM.

Message to: Olivia.

How many people do you think we'll reach?

THURS: 8:09 PM.

Message from: Oliva.

As many as possible!

I just hope people aren't rude. Elder Daniel said they usually are, but that we should try not to take it too personally.

THURS: 8:10 PM.

Our station was a new one so there were plenty of ripe fruits ready to be preached to. Other stations barely had a net difference in the people they got to convert. Most stations around universities and colleges converted international students. but in the town Oliva and I were going to, our church — the Mormon church — was new. We had only established a station there last year.

Message from: Olivia.

Are you coming to the party tomorrow? Did you hear about it? It's at school, but they're not going to play music with swear words.

THURS, 8:12 PM.

I shook my head, sighing realizing that she obviously couldn't see me. I used my fingers to push back strands of my dark hair before biting my bottom lip as I typed up a reply to her.

Message to: Oliva.

No, I'm going to stay back and look through my bags again. I'm just making sure I don't leave anything important behind.

THURS, 8:13 PM.

Message from: Olivia.

You packed like a week ago.

I was there. I helped you. What are you still sorting out? Haha.

Typing...

Do what you want though! :)

THURS, 8:14 PM.

I smiled at her text before putting my phone away and trying to carry on with what I was doing before she texted me. I worked silently, going through every inch of my box, and checking off a mental checklist. My head shot up and I looked over at my door when I heard a knock, and soon my sister, Jessica walked in her pajamas.

"When are you leaving?" Her voice was soft, and I wondered if she would miss me or if she was just worried.

"On Monday," I said. I was leaving in the middle of the afternoon with Olivia and the rest via train. Our community was a little rural farm-ing/hunting town with a population of about six thousand, and the closest town to grab a plane was three towns away.

"So, I won't see you leave?" she asked, and I just nodded in reply. She took her weight off the wall she had been leaning on before walking over to me. "Mom said there are a lot of bad people where you're going." I frowned a bit, cocking my head to the side as I looked at my sister. Sure, many people there weren't saved and didn't know the gospel and the teachings of Joseph Smith, but that's what I was going there to do — to help them learn.

"Well, when I talk to them they won't be bad people any more," I said, and that for some reason made my little sister smile. "They'll become good people," I tried to explain to my sister. A lot of people left the church from time to time. Maybe she was worried I would leave too.

"I'll pray for you, okay?" she said in an enthusiastic voice before walking away from me. I watched her leave my room, and only when the door closed quietly behind her did I look back at my luggage. Yes, everything was there and set. I guess checking just made me less anxious. I didn't even have a specific thing I was afraid of leaving behind. I was just—

Nervous.

I couldn't even pinpoint why. I ran a hand through my hair, trying to calm myself down. This will be good for me. Going will be good for me. I repeated in my mind closing my boxes before heading to sit on my queen-sized bed that was covered in a brown bedsheet. Our house was big. That was more attested to the fact that housing was cheap around here, and the house was built from scratch, than to the fact that we were rich — we weren't. My mother didn't work, and my father had a middle-class desk job. Most of the walls were done in paneling, and the floorboards were wooden too.

My parents had moved here a few years from Korea just before they had me. They hadn't been anywhere else, and I didn't really know anywhere but this small Mormon majority town. I guess that's why they were nervous.

I got up from my bed after a while of reading a bit of the novel I'd gotten a while back. There wasn't much I could read, watch or listen to. A lot of stuff was secular today, and it took a combined effort from our church's youth group and individual parents to make sure kids got entertainment that wasn't ungodly. I got out of my clothes. I had been wearing a pair of shorts and a t-shirt. I made my way to the bathroom to take a shower after that. I let my hands massage my scalp, then my face as I tried to unpack my stress and worry. I even said a little prayer as the water from the shower beat my skin.

It was going to be alright.

I will come back closer to God than ever before.

Chapter Two

The train ride was hectic and tiring. I had slept for most of it, but when we started to near the end of the trip I had woken up with a cramp in my neck. Olivia was sitting beside me reading a book, while the rest of our mates in the missionary were scattered about the train. She turned, probably realizing that I was staring at her before smiling at me. I smiled back, resting my head on the seat as I tried to get comfortable and ignore the cramp in my neck.

Olivia let out a sigh of relief when the train came to its final stop. There were some announcements from the options corner, and after a while, we were allowed to get up and leave. Olivia went about taking her backpack from the overhead compartments, while I grabbed the bag I had tossed under my seat. We woke the rest of our mates up, talking as we laughed and rubbed our tired eyes while stretching. We got down from the train, moving to check out before we eventually left the train station in general.

We were standing by the metal benches by the white building. The parking lot was just a distance away from us. The heat of the afternoon wasn't intense seeing as evening was drawing near. Our group of about fifteen were chatting amongst ourselves, our boxes scattered about as Elder Alan tried to get us to keep quiet. He was a man in his early thirties, most of us were eighteen or nineteen and would be serving in the mission for two years.

From what I heard from returning missionaries, stations were often built like tiny boarding houses with a church downstairs, and a handful of rooms to talk to people.

"I'm glad Olivia's going with you. You know most times boys leave their girlfriends behind and they come back to find them married." I blushed, remembering my mother's words. Olivia wasn't my girlfriend, and we were too young to think about marriage. Oddly enough I knew Olivia's parents brought up the marriage and dating question with her too, but we just ignored it like it was white noise in the distant background. We liked our friendship, we weren't going to give it up because of our embarrassing parents.

"I'll call for the bus," Elder Daniel said, taking out his phone before wandering away from the small group of missionaries. Most people had taken a seat on the metal chairs, while Olivia and I stood around. Like most girls in our church, she wore pantyhose along with her long flowing shirt. She was wearing a long-sleeved top, but it was loose in order for her not to feel uncomfortable with the summer heat.

We watched as people pulled their luggage and walked about with families in the parking lot while we waited. It seemed like using the train was the main transport system around here. The parking lot was filled with cabs and yellow taxis ready to pick up passengers.

"This place is huge!" Oliva commented, making me look over at her freckled face. She had braided her red hair back, allowing her round face look even more round. A smile made its way to her thin lips, and her grin exposed her pearly white teeth as she looked around the crowded parking lot. "So many people."

"Yeah..." I trailed, looking around. Yeah, there were a lot of people around. I noticed how packed together the buildings that were about the place seemed. It was quite different from how you could literally walk miles without seeing another house back home. I was in a daze when Olivia tapped my shoulder. I gasped in surprise, looking towards her before blinking.

"We're leaving," she said, pointing towards our mates that here now heading for the costar bus that had arrived for us. I let out a small 'oh' before holding on to the handles of the two boxes beside me and dragging them along with me before dropping them off with the driver who was loading the bus's trunk.

I got inside, sitting beside Olivia as usual. Before the bus driver got in and started the car Elder Daniel and brother John led us in a prayer. I closed my eyes, nodding along to the goodwill they professed into our lives. After that, we all cheered before the bus driver started the car and set up some music that we sang along to with slow claps.

Throughout the ride, I looked out the window while Olivia browsed through her phone. The evening was drawing near, and we were all getting tired. The bus stopped at a restaurant and we all ate some takeaway on the bus before leaving again. Oliva picked at my food from time to time when she finished hers, and all I could really do was roll my eyes at her while she laughed. I checked the time on my watch. It was eight in the evening now. I was starting to wonder when we would get to our missionary station.

The bus stopped at a gas station next, and I was glad since I had started to get dizzy from the moving bus.

"This will take a while. We have to change the oil, and do a brief warm-up, okay?" the bus driver said, turning back to us. His tired blue eyes looking from one corner of the bus to the other. Everyone nodded or said something in understanding before he looked away from us and got down from the bus, shutting the door to the driver's seat before heading to the mechanics' work area.

As the bus fell into slow worship songs I found myself looking out the window and towards the mechanics' place. The driver was talking to a lean dark man, as two other men went to check on the bus. I'm not sure why, but even under the dim fluorescence light covered in bugs outside, my attention was caught by the man the bus driver was talking to. He was tall, well built, and had quite a bit of tattoos if my eyes weren't deceiving me.

Tattoos.

I've actually not seen them anywhere but online before. No one in my hometown had them. It was the same way no one in town really wore makeup or did anything overly complex with their hair. Simplicity was like an unspoken rule, and modesty was ingrained in the teachings of our church and community. Half of the people that I had seen walking around since we got off from the train shocked me, and maybe staring at them for just a little bit had made me feel embarrassed, but here I was looking at this man, and it felt different, not weird or shameful. I'm not sure why.

I blinked, startled at the realization that I had zoned out. My face grew warm when I saw the man staring at me — or maybe I was just imagining things. The bus driver wasn't beside him anymore and he was leaning against the pillar with his face forward.

Is he looking at me? I wondered, not really able to tell in the dark. On a regular day, I would have looked away, and tried to forget about it, but here I was staring right back at him. More so out of curiosity than a need to stare him down. He moved away from the ceramic pillar and walked over to a different corner.

My eyes followed him.

I wasn't sure what came over me, but I wasn't resisting it. I didn't feel like resisting it.

When he walked into the light of the small work area. My eyes went wide. I could see him fully now in his plain white singlet and tattered blue jeans. I watched him take out a cigarette from his pocket before lighting it with a lighter he had retrieved from the other. The man's dark coarse hair was braided back. This time when he turned towards the bus he made eye contact with me. I hadn't been imagining things before. He had indeed been staring at me, and for some reason, I didn't mind.

"What are you looking at?" I sharply turned away from the window when I heard Olivia's voice. I turned to her, finding her staring at me with a confused frown. "Well, what were you looking at?"

"N-nothing," I stuttered, but she didn't look impressed.

"It's not right to lie, Mathew, not even little white lies," she said before looking at me and out the window. "Oh. Yikes," she simply said, and I turned to look out the window as well, and sure enough, she was looking at the same man I had been staring at.

"This town's going to be a whole lot of work, isn't it? I mean, just look at his body. He has so many tattoos, and he's smoking too," she said, and I just bit my lip. Normally I would outright agree with her, but I don't know. I didn't feel like it today — or to be more truthful, the part of me that would have reacted vilely to him was just fascinated. "Also, did you notice how most people dress around here?"

It was confusing.

"Yes," I said, answering her question. "Maybe he's just cold." I shrugged in response to her previous statement. Olivia frown before turning to me like I had grown two heads.

"But that doesn't explain the tattoos. Plus, he could wear a sweater instead of that singlet for crying out loud," she said, and I just looked away.

"I guess," I said, realizing that if I didn't reply to Olivia she might pester me later.

Did I lie again just now? I wondered, but I shook it off. Not really. It was half a lie, not a full one. I don't know. We both just stared at the man, and soon he turned towards us. Olivia looked away immediately, and I followed her lead even though I didn't actually want to.

"Gosh, he almost caught us!" she laughed, giggling. I just smiled at her, trying to distract my mind from overthinking the last few minutes by checking my phone. The bus driver hopped into the car soon after and drove out of the small clearing and back into the road.

I had a feeling of something in my chest sinking.

It was odd. Even in the midst of all the singing and cheering as we got closer to our station, I felt disappointed. But what was I disappointed about?

I don't know. I said in my head, but the image of the man smoking a cigarette filled my mind. I bit my bottom lip, deciding to shake the thought off, but it didn't work. The scene of him just standing there and smoking while he stared at me, and I stared back was all I could think about.

Chapter Three

"Hey sir, have you heard about the prophet Joseph Smith—" The door slammed shut before my partner could even finish. We both stared at the closed door in disbelief before laughing.

"Father in heaven help us," Sam said, shaking his head as he stepped down from the step. I just gave him a pitiful smile, shrugging before letting out a sigh. It was early noon, and we were asked to go out sharing filers, and asking if anyone would like to keep in touch with us.

"I should have said Jesus, everyone knows Jesus," Sam said, smacking his acne-ridden forehead as he groaned, lamenting like it was the most obvious walk around to people slamming doors shut whenever they saw us.

"But we're supposed to be teaching people about the apostasy, and our church. So yeah, we must bring up Joseph Smith at some point," I said, watching as he shrugged before adjusting his black tie. Our uniform was simple, a white long-sleeved top over black slacks and black ties. Sam's clothes were a little bit too big for him, but I guess it didn't matter much.

"Also," I started, looking out into the empty street. When we had started coming in there had been some people about, but it seemed like they disappeared into their homes to avoid us. "I don't think many people here even are Christians at all," I finished, turning back to Sam who was now nodding. Unlike most of the other towns returning missionaries spoke about, our church was the only one in sight.

"We should head back for today, maybe look around the street before ours before we do," Sam said, folding his hands. Small beads of sweat had started to form on his forehead. It was a hot day, and it was only going to get hotter if the rising temperatures were a sign of any sort. We started heading back, talking together and handing out fliers when we met people on the street. They would smile and nod their heads at us when we talked to them, but the sight of someone rolling up the flier we had given them and tossing it away right after made me feel terrible. I guess it was the same for Sam, but he kept smiling. We were doing our best after all.

"Okay, we can knock on doors in this street before heading back to the station," Sam said, stopping at the turn to the street just before ours. I hadn't really noticed this place before and we'd been at the station for about three days. I even jogged past it from time to time.

"Okay," I said, and we walked into the street, moving from house to house. For the most part, people didn't answer. Most of them pretended not to be home, but we knew better. The sound of people drawing their curtains closed and shuffling from the inside wasn't hard to miss. After a while of knocking or pressing bells, we would sigh and give up, leaving a flyer in front of the door before heading to the next house. I noticed that most of the houses here were in a conjoined building style, or they were lowly battered-looking flats.

My nose scrunched up at the smell of smoke at one person's door, but Sam persisted and continued knocking. After a few minutes of knocking and ringing the bell he stopped, and we just settled for dropping off a flyer and leaving.

"Sam," I called out as we headed for the next door. He turned to me, humming a bit before looking back at the dirt road ahead of us.

"When you smelt the smoke, you should have realized the person was a smoker. It could even be drugs, but you still knocked," I said, biting my bottom lip. I wanted to add something more to what I had said. I wanted to add that it was kind of obvious the person wouldn't want us or our preaching at his front door.

"No one's beyond saving, Mathew," he muttered in a lone tone before shaking his head like I had said something silly. We were at the next house on the street now, and we climbed the small staircase leading to the door of the flat. The building looked old and a bit unalive, like not many people lived in it.

Sam pressed the doorbell, and he seemed rather surprised when we heard the sound of someone saying they were coming to open the door without asking us who we were.

"They're going to open the door?"

"Yeah, I think so," Mathew muttered, rearranging his tie before taking out a book of Mormon and a flyer he was thinking of handing to whoever it was.

A few minutes later the door flew open, and my eyes went wide. Standing in front of the door was the man from the mechanic's repair shop. He has taken his braids out and packed his curly hair into a low puff. He stared at Sam for a while, not looking impressed before turning his gaze to me. He rose a brow, and it seemed to me that he could at least vaguely remember who I was. I looked away, staring at my black polished shoes.

"Well?" he asked after a while of all of us just standing in silence. "Is there something you want?"

"Oh," Sam suddenly said like he had come out from a daze. "We wanted to talk to you."

The man just nodded.

"I'm Elder Samuel, and here with me is Elder Mathew," Sam said, gesturing to me. I raised a hand, waving slowly, and I even dared to give the man a small smile. "We're Latter-day Saints. Err, that's the Church of Jesus Christ of Latter-day Saints, and we would love to share our ministry with you," Sam said, and the man let out a sigh before folding his hands and leaning against the edge of the door stile.

"What's your name if you don't mind sharing?" Sam asked.

"Nathaniel, most people just call me Nath for short," the man said, cracking his jaw. He was in a pair of grey jogging pants and a blue tank top.

Taking the man's silence as a permission to keep talking, Sam went ahead with the lines we were taught to say but skipping the Joseph Smith line. "Do you believe in Jesus Christ?"

"No." The man's answer was short and straight to the point.

"Well, at least you know who Jesus Christ is?" Sam asked with a nervous laugh and the man nodded, looking away for a bit to stare at the dog running by before returning his gaze to us.

"Well, what if I told you all churches apart from our church lost the ministry along the line?" Sam asked, and the man didn't give him a reaction, so he carried on. "We're the one true church."

"Every church says that," the man said plainly, smiling at us a bit before staring down at his feet. He was wearing indoor slippers. He looked bored and a little irritated, but he wasn't asking us to leave.

"Well..." Sam trailed before laughing. "If you let us in we could sit down and have a chat. We could also answer any specific questions you have."

"I don't think you want me in your church," the man said, making Sam smile a bit. "I'm gay, you're wasting your time."

"Well, it doesn't really matter we can still sit down and have a chat," Sam said, the polite smile still on his face. "We just want to share our ministry with you."

"And I'm not interested," the man said, mirroring Samuel's smile.

"Well..." Sam trailed, running a hand through his hair. "Will you at least consider taking this," Sam said, putting the book of Mormon and the flier he had in his hands forward. The man stared at it for a bit before nodding and reaching out to take it.

"Can we have your number so that we can ask you about the book?" Sam asked, and the man shook his head.

"I'm not giving you my number, this is enough," he said, waving the book in his hand before walking back into his house and shutting the door behind him.

"Well then, that went well enough, don't you think, Mathew?" Sam asked, turning towards me. I nodded, not having much to say. I had just watched the conversation play out in front of me instead of chipping in like I should have been doing.

No, I had been staring at him — at the man — at Nathaniel, as we had come to know him.

My mind was blank when we knocked on the last few doors on the street. No one else opened up for us, and we called it a day before leaving the street and heading back to the station. Sam and I shared a room, and when we got in we said a little prayer before showering and heading down for a fellowship with the rest of our mates.

There was a church downstairs as well as multiple separate rooms for fellowships. Men and women had church service together before splitting into Sunday school that was male or female-specific. Men moving to one dedicated to the priesthood, while women moving to one dedicated to sisterhood and motherhood. There were fellowships we could all attend together, and the one we were in now was one of them. A person led the fellowship, and we had a class-like setup were someone taught and we all had discussions afterword.

There were some new faces here that were probably people missionaries had convinced to come to visit us. They seemed shy, but after a while, most of them opened up and took part in the discussions. There was a step by step way we introduced potential converts to the church, and even with the gradual introduction, it was often a hit or miss.

"Mathew, concentrate," I heard Olivia scold me. I blinked, apologizing as I sat up in my seat before looking over at the chalkboard a sister in a long flowing skirt was writing on now. We were talking about the last days. It was quite a popular topic. For the life of me, I couldn't figure out why people loved talking about the end days.

"Is something wrong?" Olivia asked in a low tone, leaning into me a bit so that I could hear her in the middle of the noise in the room. It seemed like a mini-debate had broken out. I shook my head, but I wasn't being honest. I should try to stop lying. Why am I doing it more often? I asked myself as Olivia leaned away from me without asking me any more questions.

I was thinking about that man again. Wondering how he could live so close by when his workplace was far away. Or maybe it wasn't that far away, and the bus ride had just seemed unbearable long after we left the mechanics' repair shop for some reason?

I don't know, but what I did know was that I couldn't get him out of my mind. I wanted to hate that, but I just didn't.

The man had come off as cold but polite, but I could see the bitterness in his brown eyes under all that pretense of composure and calmness.

He had been more than irritated. He had been angry.

And for some reason, I wanted to know why.

Chapter Four

I t's either I was always intentionally looking for the man named Nathaniel, or he was suddenly appearing everywhere I went. Ever since Samuel and I talked to him at his door I've been seeing him taking walk whenever I went out to jog. I've also seen him at the local grocery store and feeding the stray dog that hung about this area.

Sometimes his hair was in a low or high puff, and sometimes his hair was in cornrows. He would turn to me sometimes, and I would just stare back at him until he smiled and waved at me. Only my burning cheeks and heightened heart rate ever made me look away from him. I'm not sure why I thought about him a lot. Why I was disappointed anytime I didn't see him walking about when I was jogging—

"Elder Mathew."

"Sorry?" I said, blinking before looking over at Elder Alan who was giving me a not too impressed look. He muttered something under his breath, pushing the flier on the coffee table at the center towards me. I looked down at it, picking it up before bringing it to my view.

"We're having a move movie show soon. We're looking to invite as many people around as possible to come over," he said, and I nodded. Some sisters, as well as Samuel, were in the room with us. Most of them were chatting at a corner, while a handful of us was were sitting on the sofas around the coffee table. The room was more or less an activity room and there were pictures of prophets lining the walls as well as the red curtains that covered up the windows. The ceiling was a little low here since it was the basement.

"Oh," I muttered, looking down at the fancy plan. It looked like something the sisters had thought up.

"Yes, that would get a handful of people interested in coming over, won't it?" I heard Sister Anna said, smiling widely. Her blonde hair was plaited back, making her heart-shaped face stand out.

"I'm not sure," a petite sister said, making the people around him look his way. "Think about it, the people here don't look like they'll go anywhere that doesn't have alcohol. Didn't you go to the bar with me the other day to get fried chips?" she asked, looking over at the girl who was standing behind her.

"Well, we don't have to tell them what exactly is going to go on at the party except that it's a movie showing," a sister said.

"That's lying," the petite sister said, slouching on her seat a bit as she crossed her arms over her chest. Some people around nodded in agreement, and the girl that had replied to her rolled her eyes.

"Not really, we're not just giving them any information, Marie. Loosen up."

"That's lying by omission," Marie said, and the girl groaned.

We all started laughing for some reason and went ahead with talking about the event and how to get people to come.

Later that evening I talked to my parents through email since I was only to call home twice a year. The church was still opening to a lot of things to missions. Missionaries were recently granted the right to use social media — well, just Facebook, for the most part, and it had to be for missionary purposes.

Sam arranged the corner of his room. It was a small place, with study desks and twin-sized beds on each side. My corner was mostly empty, I didn't really pack much. On the other hand, Sam had a lot of things on his bedside table and desk.

"Mathew." I turned towards Sam at the sound of him saying my name. I had just stopped communicating with my parents. I rose a brow, wondering why Sam had called me if he wasn't going to say anything. He was kneeling by his head, rearranging the drawers beneath them.

"You've been very in your head lately, did something happen?" he asked, and I found myself blinking before looking away.

Yes, something happened — actually, someone had happened. I really couldn't explain how I was feeling. "No," I ended up saying instead, and Sam just stared at me with his grey eyes. He bit his bottom lip, sighing before looking away.

I had lied again, but this time my stomach didn't feel hollow, and a sensation of wanting to throw up at my lie didn't happen. I'd been lying more frequently, and I wasn't feeling even remotely sympathetic about having to do it. It should be terrifying, but it wasn't.

It wasn't a good thing.

If only it didn't feel so necessary to do. I said to myself in my head, bringing my knees to my chest before hugging them. A good thing about being, quote in quote, 'short' meant that I didn't have to squeeze myself into a sardine to fit in the small beds we had.

"You can talk to heavenly father about whatever it is even though you don't want to talk to me," Sam said, getting up from his knees before throwing himself on his bed. His long legs exceeding the foot of the bed. He sighed, curling up into a very uncomfortable looking ball, and I laughed while he rolled his eyes at me.

Back home in the evening, the sound of chickens clucking, and rosters from different compounds crowing would have filled the neighborhood at this time. Many people back home had small poultry farms and vegetable gardens. Some had full farms as well as cows and goats for milk. We didn't eat meat much, we were asked to eat as little meat as possible. It was part of the word of wisdom.

"I'm a bit scared," Sam said after a period of silence.

"Why?" I asked, looking over at him. I watched him hum as he reached out for his book.

"What if my girlfriend's married before I get back, what then?" he asked, but I wasn't really sure if he was directing it at me per se, or if he was just airing his thoughts and needed an ear to listen.

"Well, did you propose to her before you left?" I asked, and he nodded.

"Yeah, but two years is a long time to ask her to wait," he sighed. "You're lucky that Olivia was old enough to go to the mission with you," he said, staring at me. I didn't reply to that. I wasn't sure why everyone assumed I was going to end up marrying Olivia. It made me a bit queasy too. She was even one year my senior. That was the reason why she could even attend the mission with me. Men could partake in missions when they were eighteen years and up, while women could apply when they were nineteen years and older.

A sigh left my lips as I ran a hand through my hair. Sure, we were supposed to marry early, but Sam would be twenty or twenty-one when he was done with his mission. It's not like his girlfriend would get married now. Women were only allowed to marry returning missionaries anyway, so it was now or never. I didn't say anything in reply and the room went painfully silent. Some time passed, and Sam changed the topic to keep the conversation going.

"That man from before..." he trailed, and I just stared at him.

"What man?" I asked. I mean, we've indeed been sharing a lot of pamphlets and knocking on a lot of doors, there were many men.

"That man with the err..." Sam sat up on his bed, moving his hand over his hair like he was trying to describe something big. "The man with the big hair. Well, it's not big all the time it changes quite a bit—"

"The man with the cornrows?" I asked, realizing that he was talking about Nathaniel, and for some reason, my chest felt full.

"Yes!" he said enthusiastically. People generally looked the same where we came from, and there were some few exceptions like my family, or the Thomas family down the street. It was different here. It was a melting pot of all sorts of people. So, generally, we found them hard to describe.

"Yes, him. I saw him in the grocery store the other day, and we had a nice chat," Sam said, smiling widely like he had won a victory. "I couldn't convince him to come over here though, but he's reading the book of Mormon, which is great."

I smiled, listening to Sam talk about him. Maybe he was right, maybe anyone could be saved after all.

"I've seen him around, but I haven't spoken to him," I muttered, omitting the reason why. Usually, I got flustered or bewildered by the mere sight of him.

"You should. Stay friendly, say hi. We're meant to keep up with the people we engage with, remember?" Sam said, lying on his bed before letting out a sigh. "Some people just need a little push," he said before he turned to face the ceiling, humming a worship song under his breath as I was left to just stare at him.

I blinked, hugging my pillow as I thought about it. The problem wasn't that I wasn't saying hi or interacting with him, the problem was that my mind wasn't on ministering to him. I wasn't sure what I would do or say if I was ever put in a posting where I had to talk to him, but something in my mind told me that I definitely wouldn't be preaching.

After a while, Sam got up from his bed to turn off the lights, and we were both left in darkness. I soon heard Sam's snoring, so I looked away, staring up at the ceiling.

I squinted, wondering why my mind was suddenly filled with the image of Nathaniel again. I hadn't really talked to him. I had never actually talked to him, just stared at him, but I was drawn to him unconsciously, and I didn't know what to do about it. Was it something I should worry about? Was it something I should pray for help with?

It had taken a while for me to notice that it wasn't normal. That it was weird, and he probably thought I was invasive and confused whenever he caught me looking at him.

A sigh left my lips as I shut my eyes, trying my best to push the thoughts to the back of my mind and think happy things. I felt too confused to pray. After a while of just lying in the dark, I did drift into sleep.

I thought temple garments were meant to keep your mind pure, so why was I thinking of Nathaniel? Why was the image of him smiling at and waving my way make me so confused? Why was he kissing me in my sleep?

And why did I like it?

I clenched my hands into fists when I suddenly jolted out of my light sleep. I licked the inside of my mouth as my heart beat in both fear and confusion as I recalled what happened in my dream. That's it. I concluded in my mind before covering my face with his hands. I have to talk to him.

Maybe my fascination would disappear then.

Chapter Five

The rains late last night meant that this morning was wet, dark, and cold. I was in a sweater today, and instead of jogging I was walking and doing my best not to step on any muddy puddles. That was a thing I would have to get used to since most of the roads here were dirt roads — basically, leveled earth, and nothing more.

The movie showing was planned for the evening in a few days, and most of the sisters were going to be helping with sharing pamphlets. I was mostly going to help talk to some people that had agreed to see some of the elders for the rest of the day.

I was jumping over a puddle when I heard the sound of a dog barking. My heart started to beat faster since I knew who would be with the dog.

Nathaniel? I said in my mind when I looked about the place to find him in the corner with a dog jumping about him. He was wearing a pair of jeans, and his usual tank top — very inappropriate for the weather right now. Was this a pattern? He hadn't been wearing a sweater when we visited the mechanics' place in the evening.

I bit my bottom lip, trying to decide if I should walk up to him or turn away and leave without saying anything. In the middle of fighting with myself in my head, he turned to me. I blinked, startled, but he just laughed before raising a hand in a small wave. After that, he gave the brown dog's head one last pet before making to walk away. It was then that I realized he was leaving, and I didn't give myself much time to think before I started running over to him.

"Wait!" I yelled, making Nathaniel turn to me with a startled look. Maybe he had expected me to walk away too, but here I was red-faced and wide-eyed and looking up at him.

"Well?" he asked, turning to look at me. I blinked, looking away. I knew he was tall, but I hadn't ever thought of how tall. All the times I've met him we've been standing a distance away from each other, but now that I was right in front of him I could tell how tall he was. He was taller than Sam, and Sam was 6'1.

"I..." I started, running a hand through my hair. I really hadn't thought this through. "I wanted to check up on you, have you started to read the book we gave you?" I asked, referring to the day Sam and I stopped at his house to hand him the book of Mormon and a pamphlet with the church resources written inside.

"Yes, but I already told your partner that," the man laughed, making me blink back as I watched him put his hands into his jean pockets. The morning was still cloudy, but the area was now bathed in a light blue color instead of the usual yellow.

"So, you jog every day..." the man trailed, frowning like he was trying to remember something. I watched him close his eyes, shaking his head before he opened them again. "What's your name again?" he said, probably giving up on remembering it.

"Mathew," I replied, watching as he swung his left foot about, trying to get rid of the mud that was stuck under his tennis shoes. Inappropriate shoes for the weather as well, who would have guessed? For some reason, I felt a bit insulted that he couldn't remember my name, but I shook my head, trying to remind myself that it's not like we were friends or anything.

"And you take a walk every day," I said, watching as he smiled. Now that I could see his smile up close I saw how thing it was, and how it didn't reach his brown eyes. It was like he was smiling out of politeness, for the mere fact of just smiling. That didn't sit well with me, and it made me kind of anxious. I felt like I was being treated like an inconvenience to talk to.

"Yeah, it's a good way to get you awake at seven in the morning, don't you think," the man laughed. "I have work to do, or maybe I should just stop doing the morning and night shifts," he said like he wasn't talking to me specifically.

"Oh, you do work far away?" I asked, and he shook his head. I frowned. Didn't we see him at the mechanics' workshop while we were driving to the station?

"I work around here, sometimes I do some sort of exchange, and that's why you lot saw me that night," he said with a smile as he turned and started to walk away. I was stunned, but I followed him, starting to walk at his pace when I caught up with him and was now beside him. I was in black joggers, and a blue sweater, while he was in his typical tank top. I turned to him, biting the inside of my mouth as I just watched him walk. His hair was in a low puff today, but his lips looked dry and cracked. I wondered if he was cold, but I didn't ask.

"So, how's your..." the man trailed as if looking for the right word to say. "How's your church stuff been going," he ended up saying instead, making me laugh.

"It's been fine," I answered, stepping out of the path of a puddle before moving to walk beside him again. "We're having a movie showing soon. It's more or less a party, do you want to come?"

"I'm not the one for parties," Nathaniel said rolling his eyes as he took his hand out of his pocket again. "Also, stop trying to get me into your church. I'm not interested," he said, and I looked away, realizing that from his tone I had probably touched a nerve. I bit my bottom lip, deciding to say something despite my better judgment.

"But you're reading the book. That must mean something, right?" I asked, watching as he chuckled.

"It means that I love books, nothing more nothing less," he said. I frowned a bit. I hadn't thought of him as the type that would like reading, but I guess that was a subconscious bias of mine, nothing that really had to do with him per say. I mean, I didn't know him much, and this was the first time we were actually exchanging words.

"Oh," I simply said, and he chuckled.

"Anyone can be saved," I said. "You can just sit with up and discuss things," I added, looking over at him. His face had a small frown now like he was irritated. He rolled his eyes, scratching the back if his neck before sighing.

"You are kind of cute, but that's enough of a bribe to get me chained in a room with you lot," he said, making my eyes go wide as I looked away.

Why did he say that? What does he mean by that?

"So, let's say I join you all for a talk. Then we do it again, and we do it again," he started before staying quiet. The sound of our feet treading on the soft soil soon filled the void before he decided to finish what he has started saying. "Let's say I keep saying yes, what happened when my gayness is brought up?" Gayness. The way he said it made me look away. He was laughing now, but was it at himself or at me?

"What happens then?" he repeated when I didn't say anything in reply.

"Well..." I trailed before closing my mouth and deciding not to say anything.

"So, you're not going to tell me about the whole how you respect everyone, but you'll hope that I 'change', hmm?" he asked, his voice had gone cold like he wasn't talking to m but someone else in the distance. The bitterness I had spotted before was oozing out of him now, and that made me realize that he had probably been trying to restrain himself before.

"There's a thing about tolerance," he started, moving his hand to fiddle with the small necklace around his neck, but on closer inspection, I noticed it wasn't a necklace — a rosary? "Everyone thinks it's a fancy neutral word, but it really isn't. It's more like, how do I explain this? You can't weed a particular plant in your garden, so you just leave it there — tolerate it, until you get the chance to. You might never get your way, you might never have the opportunity to do what you want, but that mindset still sticks. You're 'tolerating' it. You don't really want it there."

Our head for our mission had told us about people hurting during the training. He had said it would take a long time to get through to people, especially when it was personal. We got outbursts when we talked to LGBT+ people, other Christians when we told them they haven't really been part of a real church, sometimes women and people in premarital relationships. I looked up at Nathaniel again. It was personal. It was obvious to me, and now I plain sight. He was no longer the calm presenting person he had been his door.

I bit my bottom lip. I knew what would happen, but saying it would sound rude? I had to treat a discussion like this with care, that why we didn't confront people about these things until later on when we spoke to them, because it was personal, and a hard thing to give up.

Nathaniel just laughed, shaking his head as we continued to walk in the silence. It was getting brighter, and I started to wonder how long we had been walking. My eyes went wide when I realized I was just following him and I really didn't know where we were heading. I paused, and he stopped to look at me.

"I have to leave," I said, and he just shrugged as he watched me turn and jog away. I didn't really care if I was getting mud on my joggers, I just needed to make it back on time.

A sigh of relief left my lips when I got to the building and headed upstairs. Sam wasn't awake yet, so I took a shower and reflected on what had happened just a few minutes ago. I had talked to Nathaniel like we were old pals taking a jog together. It both confused and intrigued me. The memory of my dream last night soon filled my mind, and I was blushing uncontrollably.

I stared at the mirror, holding my face. Is it because he called me cute? I wondered, shaking my head as I started to mutter a successive string of 'no's. No, I was just overwhelmed with our conversation. That was all, nothing more, nothing less. It wasn't that I was fascinated with him. It wasn't that his looks made my eyes linger too long.

It was that I was trying to reach out to him — handling a difficult case — that was it.

Although I said that to myself my previous thought kept hanging around in my head like background music. It was like it was poking fun at me and raveling in my distress.

It was of the devil.

It wasn't normal.

I won't let it be normal.

Chapter Six

It was early noon, and I was sitting in with Sam and brother Joshua to have a chat with one of the people Joshua and his partner had convinced to come and sit down with us. She was a tall woman and looked like maybe she was somewhere in her twenties. We were in one of the many small rooms built for this exact purpose in our station. Joshua was talking, carrying out the lesson like we had been taught to.

"So, there's no hell?" the lady asked, looking over at Elder Joshua who had just finished speaking. I nodded, before sighing and shaking my head when I realized the girl wasn't looking at me.

"Yes, there's no hell. Heavenly Father loves us so much that the worst place he could put us in is a world like the one we live in now," I said, watching as the lady with pale skin and dark hair looked over at me. She smiled, rubbing her eyes that had dark circles under them — she seemed amused.

"Then why all this?" she asked, and I frowned a bit, looking from her to Joshua and then at Sam.

"Why what?" Sam asked, adjusting his position in his chair.

"Well, if you're not going to get punished for being a bad person, and if you're a good person you still get a good place to stay..." she trailed, pausing a bit like she was trying to remember what she had told. "The terrestrial kingdom, that's what you called it, wasn't it?" she asked and we all nodded our heads. She smiled, folding her hands.

"So, if there's no hell, what's the point of being Christian? What's the point of living so strictly like you have a stick up your ass?" she asked, and I coughed into my hand, trying to stop the laugh that had formed in my throat from spilling over. People here did have potty mouths.

"Well, human beings long to be reconnected with the father—"

"Well, I don't," she said, cutting Joshua off. I just stared blankly at her, but I spotted Sam shaking his head from the corner of my eye.

"So, we strive for completeness, completeness only a connection with heavenly father will give you," he said opening up the pamphlet on the table. "Also, wouldn't it be sad to be resurrected, and then find that you could have lived in a world filled with no pain and suffering if you had followed the gospel here on earth?"

The lady slouched on the couch, tapping her fingers on the arm of the chair. "I'm not sure. I kind of like my life as it is now," she said, and Joshua just smiled. "Besides, you said that people preach to, and covert dead people before judgment day. Why can't I just give my life to heavily father there? When I'm sure he exists."

Joshua chucked a bit, holding his hands together as he nodded. He looked like he was trying to search for how to explain things in better detail to her. He tapped the fabric of his trousers before running a hand through his dirty blonde hair. I could tell that he was getting a bit frustrated with her, but like with everything else — patience was key, so we sat there with her for another half hour before calling it a day.

"People are strange," Sam told me as we left the room and walked upstairs to our room. We had service in about two hours, so we had to get ready. I couldn't see his face since I was walking behind him, but I knew he was fuming. He only walked this fast when he was. "Imagine not wanting to have happiness that's beyond description? She said she likes her life now. Did you see her eyes? It looks like she takes drugs."

I wanted to ask him how he knew that, and whether he wasn't just saying things because he was annoyed with the way she was reacting. Sure, she might as well be trolling us, but at least she had come to talk to us. That was more than a lot of people would do.

"Yeah." I just nodded in agreement with him before retreating back to the worries in my head.

It was early in the evening and a handful of us had come outside to share fliers. Church service had ended a few minutes ago, and it had made me smile to see some new faces in the crowd. It seems some people had been convinced to come for a sit-in.

I was walking side by side with Olivia, watching her flash smiles to absolute strangers, and getting them to listen to her talk about our church and the party we were holding soon. A smile spread across my face as I watched her talk to them. She'd always been able to be convincing and bubbly, so it didn't faze me that she got more hits than misses.

"We should go down this path," she said, turning away from the person she had handed a pamphlet to look at me, making her red flowing shirt to sweep across the air with the movement. She was now pointing towards a narrow dirt road that I've never visited before, but I nodded, concluding that Olivia knew what she was doing.

After a few minutes of walking, we saw a couple of small shops positioned in front of small homes and buildings. Olivia smiled, making me follow her as she quickened her steps. She started heading from shop to shop, handing out fliers before meeting me at the road pavement so we could walk up ahead.

"Oh, look! There's a shop there!" she said, smiling brightly before walking ahead of me. I rolled my eyes. I was exhausted and tired of walking around, but Olivia looked like she was having the time of her life. Maybe I should ask about her secret to being enthusiastic.

I eventually caught up with her, but I lagged behind a bit. The area caught my eye when I realized that there were mainly cars around. We had either gotten to a car repair shop or some automobile dump of some sort. My theory of it being a car repair shop was confirmed after I looked around and turned to find Olivia heading over to a large open shed. She went in and immediately started talking to the person inside.

I made my way to the shed, and when I got closer, I could tell who exactly Olivia was talking to. It was Nathaniel. His hair was in a man bun, or whatever it was called. As usual, he was wearing a tank top over trouser bottoms. He had mentioned working close by during our walk.

I headed closer to the shed before I leaned on the door. Apart from Olivia who was now inside the shed with him, he seemed to be the only person working here at the moment. My heart started to beat more quickly as I watched them exchange words. I bit my bottom lip as I tried not to appear panicked. Since the day I walked with Nathaniel in the morning I had avoided him like the plague for obvious reasons, but now, I couldn't just turn around and pretend I didn't see him. Olivia was here, and she would ask me what was going on. I didn't plan to tell anyone about the thoughts I've been having lately. I wanted to resolve those feelings — whatever they were — on my own.

"Look, you can ask him," I heard Nathaniel say, turning to gesture at me with his outstretched hand. My eyes went wide. I hadn't realized they had noticed me standing here. My eyes moved to the floor that was littered with screws and scrap metal. What did he tell her? I had zoned out while they were talking, and I was starting to get a bit worried.

What if—

"He says you've already told him about the party, is that correct?" Olivia asked, turning her round freckled face towards me. I nodded in response, calming down considerably. Thank goodness. I said in my mind. But if I had to be honest with myself, what was I expecting? I wasn't even sure why I had been panicking. They were my feelings, it's not like Nathaniel knew I had them, so he couldn't tell someone. I was just being anxious.

"Yes, I did," I said, and Olivia nodded, letting out a sigh. With that she walked away from Nathaniel's side, biting her bottom lip as she tried to think of what to do now.

"Sir, I'm leaving this filer..." she trailed off, looking around the small place filled with tools, and scrap. She was holding the brightly colored filer in her hand. The smile she had been wearing all day widened when she spotted a table, and she walked over to it, placing the flier right on top. "Right here. Please don't throw it out," she said, finishing her previous sentence. Nathaniel laughed.

It was a nice laugh. Filled with amusement, not irritation or frustration.

"Anything you want, pretty lady," he said before disappearing into the raised old car that he had been raising with a jack while Olivia was looking around. Olivia chuckled shaking her head before she walked over to me and tapped my shoulder.

"You've just been staring," she whispered, smiling before walking past me and out of the shed. I blinked, still standing there. After a while I left the shed too, catching up with Olivia before we started walking back to our station. It was evening now, about five in the afternoon. The sun was still out, but clouds had started to gather, making the hot day cooler. My mind wandered off to Nathaniel when I saw the dog he would usually feed run past us.

Pretty lady? I wondered, remembering what he had called Olivia back in the shed. A small frown made its way to my face. Why would he say that? I wanted to believe that I was mad because he was being inappropriate, but thoughts of him calling me cute that day on our walk kept flooding my mind. I wasn't furious for Olivia. I was jealous on my behalf. My esteem was crushed by the fact that he might have just been messing around that morning. It had also suffered a little blow when I realized he didn't even seem a bit upset with me for avoiding him. Wasn't that what I wanted? Why was I upset? It was confusing and slightly terrifying.

I tried to zone out of my mind. I talked to Olivia as we walked back to the station. I offered to help the sisters in the kitchen even though I wasn't supposed to be there and ended up sitting alone in the empty chapel room trying to pray, but my prayers were lost in a sea of confusion and panic.

Chapter Seven

<hr>

The morning sun was out early today, so the empty streets were flooded in a warm yellow-blue color as I made my regular morning jog. My head was throbbing, and my legs were tired, but I kept jogging anyway. For the past week, I've been overworking myself — keeping myself as busy as possible in order not to let my mind stray too far. I still saw Nathaniel around the place. In the grocery store, taking walks or talking to other people. He would wave at me when he saw me sometimes, but most times when he was with someone he wouldn't acknowledge me. It made me upset, but that was what I wanted. I didn't want him being too friendly with me, right?

my breathing gave way and I eventually stopped in my tracks, bending over to hold my burning knees as I tried to recover my breath. The soles of my feet were burning inside my shoe, and it felt like someone was banging two plates on my face simultaneously. Well, jogging hadn't cleared my mind, that's for sure.

"Are you trying to commit suicide by exhaustion?" a voice asked, making me hold my already labored breathing. I looked up to find Nathaniel looking down at me with a not too impressed look on his face. How had he gotten here? How hadn't I noticed someone was walking up to me?

He soon looked away with a sigh, and I watched as he searched the sling bag he had on him before taking out a bottle of water.

"This was for me, but since you're practically dying, you can have it," he said, stretching out the plastic bottle. "Come on, take it before I change my mind," he said, and I heaved, taking the bottle from him before muttering a small 'thank you.'

"You've been avoiding me," he said, making me choke on the water I had started to drink. I heard his laughter ring through the street as I hit my chest and tried to recover from the water in my throat. I closed the bottle with its cap before turning over to look at him. He was now smiling with a raised full brow as he stared at me. I looked away, not knowing exactly what to do. I looked up after a while like a guilty child caught coloring on the desk.

"I thought you were trying to show me the light?" he asked, putting an emphasis on the last word by making quotation marks with his fingers. I looked away again, and when I looked up he had his hands crossed, and he was looking at me with a mix of what looked like amusement and curiosity. "What happened?" he asked, making me shift on the spot.

I looked away again, scratching the back of my neck as I tried to think of what to tell him. I didn't want to lie to him. I had managed to curb that habit that had popped out of nowhere, but I didn't want to tell him what was really in my mind. It was too personal, and essentially not his business in any way. Plus, it was embarrassing.

A laugh came from him again, and I looked at him. He was still smiling. He shook his head, sighing as he tucked his hands into his pockets. Unlike the rest of the times I've seen him, he was wearing a sweater today. The weather didn't call for it today, though. It was reasonably warm outside. Weird. That was the only way I could define the long-sleeved grey sweater. It looked out of place on him since it covered most of his tattoos.

"Aren't you going to tell me why you've been playing cat and mouse with me?" he asked, making me blink before muttering an apology and scratching the back of my neck. I hadn't even noticed I had been staring at him without saying anything.

"I..." I trailed, and he looked on as I cocked my head to the side.

"Well, if you don't want to tell me just tell me that. Tell me that you don't want me to know. It's that simple," he said, and I blinked at his words, staring straight at him with wide eyes. He smiled down at me, clicking his tongue before kicking a stray stone on the ground. "You're too polite to say what I suggested, and you're too afraid to lie. You're funny," he went on to say when I didn't say anything in reply. I ended up looking away and turning my gaze to the brown earth. He was right in that regard, and I didn't know what to feel about that.

"How was the party?" he asked me as he started to move. I looked on at him, thinking about it for a bit before I made to catch up to him.

"It was okay," I said, watching as he nodded. I noticed that he had his hair in a low puff today, and he was wearing the rosary like last time. The station had hosted the movie showing in the backyard of the building a few days ago. It had been in the evening, and a handful of people had shown up. We had used the chance to talk to some of them. The party served its purpose.

"How's the pretty lady?" he asked, referring to Olivia. I felt my mind go blank for a bit before I frowned a little. Why was he asking about her?

"Woah there, soldier. I'm just asking. What are you, her father?" he laughed, and a feeling of shame wash over me. More so because that wasn't the reason I had been frowning. My worry was attached to jealousy, not an inert feeling to protect my friend. That was what I should have felt, not jealousy.

Nathaniel started to hum as we came towards a narrow path. I would often see him disappear at this point anytime I saw him while taking my walks, but now I was following him. The road had a very narrow clearing which pointed to the fact that it was caused by the treading of feet and not a conscious effort to clear a road.

"Do you..." I found myself trailing, not exactly sure of what I was trying to ask. Nath turned to me with a raised brown on his face. I just shook my head, and we continued to walk. Maybe the silence that was only tinted by the sound of birds singing in the distance made me nervous. Being close to the man that was at the center of my worries also made me a bit agitated. It was confusing. I was both happy to see him and terrified that my feelings would taunt me in full force even after we separated. He had a way of lingering in my mind.

"Do I what?" he ended up asking after some time passed. I kept my eyes on the road, not turning to look at him. The path had become a bit rocky — filled with small rocks and peddles, and I could hear some frogs which meant that there was probably water nearby.

With a shrug, I let out a sigh. I had wanted to ask him something, but it had been a fog of a question in my head at that moment, but now that I knew what I had wanted to ask him I felt embarrassed by it. Would I be prying too much if I asked him about his relationship status? Why did I even want to know his relationship status?

"Nothing's off bounds," he said, making me turn my head to him. He sounded like he was tempting me, giving me a little push. "You can ask me anything, church boy."

Okay. he just likes bad nicknames. I concluded in my mind, laughing as he rose a brow at me. I shook my head before muttering an apology for laughing under my breath. "I wanted to ask if you were seeing someone. You know..." I shrugged hoping that he understood. He chuckled, looking on at me with amusement. His smile seemed to widen, but I couldn't figure out what was going on in his head.

"No." His answer was blunt and straight to the point, and I just nodded, hugging myself as I bit my bottom lip. Why do I feel relieved? I knew why. I just didn't want to admit it to myself. Pretending to be oblivious felt safer.

"You?" I was caught off guard by that, but I still answered with a shake of my head. I wasn't dating anyone, and to be honest, I hadn't ever really thought about it. Most people just assumed Olivia was my girlfriend. The walk soon went silent, and the only noise filling the air was the sound of moving trees, our shoes treading on the ground and the irritating croaking, chirps and stridulating coming from frogs, birds, and bugs.

"Why do you wear a rosary?" I found myself asking as Nathaniel came to a stop by the small stream. It wasn't a stream exactly. It was more of an artificial lake caused by the nearby damn. I watched as he shrugged, moving his fingers to the wooden rosary around his neck.

"For keep's sake," he said, bending down to pick a small peddle before tossing it into the lake. It hopped across the green-blue water for a while before sinking with a plop sound. "My ma was very religious," he said, and I looked over at him with a questioning gaze.

"Was?"

"Not was as in dead. Was as in she's no longer religious," he laughed, and I felt a bit bad for assuming the worst.

"Oh," I said running a hand through my dark hair. Nath chuckled again, looking away from me and towards the water. We stood there, side by side not saying anything to each other for a while. Nathaniel started whistling, and soon he was humming a song under his breath. I looked at him from the side of my eye. He looked at peace, and it was strangely satisfying to just stare at him.

"You look at me a lot," he said, making my eyes go wide before I looked away. My cheeks warmed up at being caught, and soon his laughter filled the air in the area.

"I'm sorry about that," I said, covering my face. "Gosh, I'm so sorry."

"It doesn't matter," he laughed, and I heard his footsteps approached me. "Maybe I even like it," he said, startling me. When I took down my hands away from my face I looked up to find him towering over me. Just staring down at me with a small smile on his face.

"You're odd," he said as his smile widened a bit.

Is that a good thing? I wondered as a frown took form on my face. He looked like he was about to say something, but he stepped away, turning before walking away from me. He walked over to the water, staring into it as he bit his bottom lip.

"You should be going, it's almost eight-thirty," he said, looking down at his watch on his wrist. I blinked, looking down at mine and panicked when I confirmed that that was the case.

"Just walk up the path and you should be fine from there!" His voice was raised, and loud. So much so that I could still hear it echo as I ran as fast as I could, leaving him behind in the small almost surreal pocket of land he had brought me to.

Chapter Eight

To: JiHeePark@gmail.com

Subject: I just thought I should write home.

Hello mum, it's Mathew. I've been at the station for about one month now, and I thought I should message you. Everyone here in the station's doing alright. We're having a lot of fun and learning a lot along the way.

How's everyone? I hope Cath and Jessica are doing okay. Please ask them to pray for me.

I need it. I thought to myself as I typed up an email to my mother. For the past few days, I had been taking walks with Nathaniel and learning more about him. Now I knew Nathaniel still visited the Catholic church in the town that was a few hours ride from the one we were in. I also knew Nathaniel didn't talk to his father — or didn't know him. I wasn't too sure about the exact details.

I bit my bottom lip as I stared at my screen My chest started to feel a bit tight. What if they knew? I wondered, thinking to my parents. This was something I had started panicking about. I started thinking about how Olivia would react, how my brothers would react, how my small little town back home would react if they found out that I was thinking about a man like this. Though it was just plain paranoia, it's not like anyone could see my thoughts written on my face.

I had feelings for Nath, and worse still, I had stopped fighting them. I was banking on the chance that Nath himself would never notice and they would fade away with time, but I had two years in this station, and I wasn't too confident that I wouldn't do something stupid before then. I was already jealous of everyone and everything that hung around Nath that I might as well implode from the feeling of jealousy alone.

I let out a sigh, allowing my fingers to meet with the keys of my laptop.

I've been enjoying my service. I thought it was going to be hard, to be honest, but it's a lot like repeating the training we got back home. Sam and I are talking to a few people at the moment and helping them out with the basics. It's nice to help people find a path to God.

As you stray from yours. A voice said in my head as I continued to type up the email. I ignored it, trying my best to concentrate on the wall of text in front of me.

Olivia's a natural at this. She's doing great. I don't think she has written to home yet. I should remind her to do that.

I continued in my email. It was early in the morning. About four A.M. to be exact. I wasn't going downstairs for my regular jog until seven, and I don't even think I wanted to go. Nath had told me he was going out of town to the other shop he worked at sometimes. He had even handed me his house keys, 'just in case.' I wasn't sure what that meant. Was he trying to lead me into doing something? Was he expecting something from me?

God, I'm overthinking this.

My worries clouded my thoughts, and I couldn't really concentrate on writing the email. I saved it as a draft before getting up from the seat at my study desk. Sam was still out like a rock, and probably won't be awake until eight-thirty.

After some time of just sitting around, I got up and headed downstairs, deciding that I would go for a walk after all. I started slowly on the street with our station on it, but I increased my pace as I jogged through the street that led to the path Nathaniel often took. I smiled when I spotted the stray dog. It was sitting at its usual corner, probably waiting for Nathaniel. It was a shame that the man wasn't around to hand him treats today.

"He's a sweetheart," I remembered the woman that ran the local grocery store saying as I had come to buy some bread. Nathaniel had just left the store from the back of the shop. He had helped her move her things around. "It's a shame he doesn't talk much. I wonder why." I had just smiled at her words as she handed me the plastic bag with the loaf of bread in it. It seemed Nathaniel was well known, and not known at all at the same time. He seemed to be leaving small footprints everywhere he went, seeming more like an experience than a solid person. I wondered why he was like that. Maybe that was just his nature, and I was overthinking things like I usually do.

I wanted to know more about him, but he was reserved, and I didn't want to seem intrusive and poke nosy. It didn't help that I had dropped everything about church and God. My brain was too tired to be spiritually active for myself, not to talk of someone else.

When I started to accept the fact that my feelings crossed the line of mere fascination, I started to see him differently, and I wanted to know more about him. I had stopped avoiding him. I had started taking walks with him in the morning and talking to him when I could, but he treated me like he treated everyone else. With a smile on his full lips and an interaction filled with light conversation that never really crossed the line of discussing anything besides the mundane. A few times it would become personal, and he would leave or make me leave by pointing out the time.

I pat the sides of my grey jogging pants, feeling my keys as well as Nath's keys in them. I still wondered why exactly he had given them to me. Was he playing mind games, or did I just wish he was? When I had asked yesterday on our walk he had just shrugged and said, 'just in case.' In case of what? Was the question I've been asking myself since yesterday afternoon. I had zoned out during two meetings, and I had spent a lot of time just holding the keys in my hands as I lay in bed that night.

A sigh left my lips as I slowed down and began walking. I made it into the narrow path, and as usual, the croaking of frogs, and the sound of birds singing and jumping from branch to branch filled the air in the area. I soon got to the clearing by the stagnant lake created by the dam. This was more or less Nathaniel's thinking ground, and it had become mine too since it became a habit to follow him during his walks.

"What's happening?" I asked out loud, listening as my voice rang through the area. I stared down at my blurry reflection in the blue-green river, shaking my head before looking up again. What am I doing? I thought to myself as I ran my fingers through my hair, feeling the strands slip through and fall back. I really didn't know what I was doing.

I took Nath's keys out of my pocket before holding them in a fist, feeling the cool metal of the keys press against my skin. "He gave them to me because he trusts me, right?" I asked myself out loud, trying to hold on to any reason that meant I was special in some way. I wanted to be special to Nath. The man that had made himself simple yet complex. It was like I could see bits of him through a beaded curtain, and the simple glimpses only made me want to see the full picture.

My dreams.

He had more than made himself at home there. Sometimes he would kiss me, and sometimes I would just watch on as he did simple tasks. Images of his lips curling into a smile, and his dark eyes looking at me with amusement filled my mind. Also, his tank tops. His stupid tank tops. A smile spread across my face as my laughter filled the air. Is this what a crush was supposed to feel like? I wouldn't know. I hadn't had one before. A frown soon replaced the smile on my face as I started to think about what I had gotten myself into. I had allowed this to happen. I had given up on trying to ignore it and just let it run amok.

Yet I wasn't satisfied.

It was like greed had started to build up in me. I wanted something more, but I was too afraid to reach out for it. Maybe I did hope that he would reach out to me, so I wouldn't feel guilty for doing it myself, but it seemed like he might not even take a liking to me. This was not what I had expected to happen at all. I had wanted things to fizzle out, but why did I now feel restless because nothing was happening? This was one-sided. I should be happy that was the case, but I wasn't.

Dangerous. That's what my thoughts were, but I didn't seem to care anymore. I woke up, repeated prayers and duties more like a teacher than a believer. I wasn't sure if the gravity of my thoughts and sins that were weighing on me was what was causing this recoil. I was letting it happen, there was no excuse for that, and the worst part was that I didn't mind. I didn't want my feelings to go away anymore.

What was this? Jealousy, greed, envy — just too many to list, and I was too exhausted from overthinking. Maybe this is how people so deep in sin felt okay with just living in it. Mine were not even manifested into actions yet, and I was already numb. I want more, so I am going to reach out for more. The conclusion I made in my mind all of a sudden filled me with newfound energy. Suddenly the screws started turning in my head, and I was thinking up scenarios when I would get some time with Nathaniel, and maybe hint to him how I felt.

He said he likes books, then maybe I should get him books. I bought some of my favorite books along with me, but I highly doubt he would like them He didn't seem like the type that would like Christian fantasy. I kept thinking of how to tell him how I felt without actually telling him. Yes, it seems like doing things in circles was my style.

I stood by the lake with my hands in the pockets of my joggers as dwelled in my thoughts. Some time passed before I checked my watch to see that it was almost eight, so I left the clearing and started heading back to the station. The dog was still lying down on the ground when I passed it.

"He'll be back tomorrow, don't worry," I said with a smile, walking past the confused dog. It stood up, making a sound between a whine and a bark before settling down on the earthen floor again. A chuckle escaped my lips as I continued on my way.

Yes, Nathaniel would be back tomorrow, and I would pay him a visit — to return his keys of course.

Gosh, who was I kidding?

Chapter Nine

I was standing in front of Nathaniel's house now. I just stared at the door, feeling the confidence that had built up in me a few hours ago simply drain out of my system. I had an excuse as to why I was here — returning his key, but it was a weak one. He could easily get it from me during his regular morning walks when we met up. A sigh left my lips as I ran a hand through my hair. I had lied to get out of the station, saying I was visiting someone I had started staying in touch with. Well, it was more of a half-lie. I wasn't here to talk about God with Nathaniel, that's for sure.

From what the lady at the grocery store told me, he had come back earlier today. It was early noon now, I hadn't seen him since he came back, so here I was.

My eyes went wide when my ears picked up the sound of the door lock turning. I stood frozen, watching as the wooden door flew open and Nathaniel stepped out. He didn't notice me at first, but when he did one of his brows rose up as he gave me a confused look.

"I came to return your keys," I said, looking away from him as I searched my pockets for his keys. When I found it, I took it out before walking over to him and stretching it out to him. He hesitated a bit before taking the key from my open palm.

"Is that all you wanted to do?" he asked.

No. Of course, I didn't say that out loud. Instead, I just stared at him with my lips lightly parted like I had lost my voice. He chuckled, shaking his head before moving to drop the garbage bag he was holding in the bin by the door. He walked into his house, holding his door open before staring at me.

"Are you coming?" he asked, and I blinked, nodding before walking into his house as well. He closed the front door behind us, and it was then it dawned on me that I was really inside his house. My eyes darted from corner to corner, taking in the small living room we were standing in now. The place was simple with the basic colors and furnishing. Exactly what I had expected. Nathaniel had struck me as the simple type of person.

"Do you want anything to drink?" I heard him ask as I watched him head towards the tiny kitchenette at the corner.

"Yeah, water is fine," I said, watching as he hummed, opening the tiny fridge before pulling out a pack of juice instead.

"How's this?" he asked, waving it above his head so I could see it.

"It's fine," I answered, wondering if he hadn't heard me ask for water, but I didn't think about it too much.

I stood around, watching as he went about filling out a glass for me. I thanked him when he brought it to me and started to drink from the glass as he went ahead to take a seat on one of the beaten-up sofas.

"So," he started, reaching out for the remote on the coffee table in front of him. "What are you here for?" he asked, looking over at me. I paused drinking the orange juice, and just stared at him, trying to think up what to say.

"I came to return your keys."

"We both know you're lying Math," he said, and I just stared at him with wide eyes.

Math.

He had never called me that before. The room fell into silence and we just stared at each other until Nath gestured for the seat beside him. I took that as an invitation to sit down so I went ahead and did just that. The sofa sank a bit with my weight, and I let my fingers hit the glass slowly as I tried to avoid his gaze. It felt like he was boring holes into my head.

"I know why you're here," he said, making my head shoot up to stare at him. Did he really? I wondered, watching as a hint of a smile formed on his lips. "But I can't really do anything if you don't make the first move, you see." His laughter then filled the room, and I wasn't sure how to feel. My face grew warm, and my hands were a bit shaky. Afraid that I would drop the glass I placed it on the side table by the sofa I was sitting on.

The room went quiet again, and then Nathaniel suddenly stood up. "Do you want to take a look at my books?" he asked, and I just stared at him.

"Books?"

"You know I like books, why do you look so shocked?" he asked, shaking his head as he turned around and started leaving. I got up, walking quickly so that I could catch up to him. He led me through the small hallway, and soon we were in a small study with about three bookcases. Nath wandered over to the desk at the corner, sitting on it before spreading out his hands like he was presenting the room to me.

"Take a lot around," he said, and I turned to the closest bookcase, looking through the titles.

"You know, I wanted to get you a book," I started, trying to get rid of the piercing silence the room had fallen into, " but I couldn't really tell what you would like," I added before looking over at him with my hands in the pockets of my trousers. "I don't know you too well."

I watched him raise a brow at me before chuckling. "So, you want to know me?" he asked, and I looked on at him with a surprised gaze before I eventually nodded, answering honestly. There was a lot I wanted to ask him, but at the same time, I didn't want to give myself away or sound too nosey.

"I like memoirs," he started, swinging his legs. He was wearing pale blue jeans that fitted him nicely. I looked away, closing my eyes and saying a tiny prayer in my mind. Yes, I had been detached from praying for a while, but Nathaniel running around in my mind was one of the few reasons I closed my eyes and asked for God's interference. "And I like theology."

"Oh," I said in reaction to the last bit. He smiled, swinging his legs as he hummed.

"What else do you want to know about me?" he asked, and I shrugged, moving closer to him. I made sure to stay about a foot away, not wanting to be too close.

"Why don't you live with your mother?" I asked, and I watched him freeze for a bit, probably wondering if he should tell me. I watched him sigh before he ran a hand through his hair that he had put in twists today.

"She kicked me out," he said, and my eyes went wide.

"Oh." My response was flat and lame. I knew it, but I had nothing more to say. I hadn't thought about the possibility at all. He didn't seem phased by it, or even angry. If my parents kicked me out I would probably have cried until I died from exhaustion, but here he was, mentioning it like it was a passing fact.

"Your dad?" I asked, and he bit his lip, shaking his head.

"I really don't know where he is," he laughed. The laughter was tainted with nervousness, and what sounded like pain. Unlike with his mother, he seemed affected by this, and it made me a bit curious, but I didn't ask him about it any further. He didn't look like he wanted to talk about it.

"I have two little sisters," I said, moving the conversation to me, trying to do away with the awkwardness I had created. He looked over at me with a raised brow, probably wondering why I had shared such a random fact with him. I smiled at him, and he smiled back before looking away. "I asked them to pray for me," I said, laughing at myself. I'm not sure why it sounded so ridiculous all of a sudden.

"How are the prayers working out?" Nathaniel asked me, and I looked up to him, walking over the foot of distance I had kept between us. Soon I was leaning on the desk beside his sitting figure, looking right into his dark eyes.

"Not well to be honest," I said, and his smile returned. My chest was starting to get butterflies, and my mind was fogged as I watched his lips move. I blinked, watching as he created space between us on the desk, moving so that my hands were no longer too close to him.

"I usually don't mess around with people who are still in the closet," he said, making me open my mouth before closing it.

Still in the closet. I repeated in my mind. There was a mist in my mind and a slight panic. I had only just dawned on me that the word 'gay' might apply to me and that I would eventually have to do that coming out thing Nathaniel was talking about.

"Is something wrong?" his voice was a muffle within my mind as I started thinking about things. My mind had been on Nathaniel and Nathaniel alone. I hadn't really thought of what my attraction meant. I hadn't thought about how it probably meant I was gay.

"Are you okay?" I heard his voice again, and this time I also felt his hands on my shoulder. I blinked, looking up as I was turned to face him. "Are you okay?" he repeated, and I nodded when he gave me a little shake.

"I'm sorry. I w-was just thinking," I mumbled, not really knowing how to explain myself.

"About being gay?"

"About being gay," I replied honestly, and he just sighed, letting go of my shoulders before folding his hands over his chest.

"So, what about it?" he asked, and I just shrugged.

"I don't know. I wasn't really thinking of anything beyond the present," I admitted, and Nathaniel's smile returned.

"Your church, your friends, your family... You weren't thinking about them?" he asked, and I shook my head. Of course, I had been thinking about them, but never really in the grand scale detail that had happened a few seconds ago.

"I was," I said out loud, "Not just overwhelmingly if that makes sense," I said, and Nathaniel just frowned at me.

"Then what do you want to do?" he asked, and I just stared at him. I wasn't sure what was happening, what this whole situation meant. Did he like me as I liked him? Was he just entertaining me? What in the world was going on? I bit my bottom lip, running a hand through my dark hair as I stared down at the carpeted floor.

"I'll tell you what," he said, making me look back up at him. He had moved back to the desk, and his back was resting on it. "If you make a move I won't push you back," he simply stated. "And if you decide to back off I won't chase you."

With a mind full of lust and confusion I moved forward, walking until I had to stop right in front of him. He towered over me.

"I want to kiss you," I said.

"Reasonable," he replied, looking down at me, his full lips twisting into a smile.

"I haven't kissed anyone before," I confessed, and his eyes seemed to widen in interest, but I ignored him, continuing with what I have to say. "I can't make the first move, so if you could kiss me—"

I didn't get to finish because he hand leaned off the table to pull me to himself. I hadn't been this close to anyone in my life. I imagined being pressed against someone like a sardine to be uncomfortable, but now that my body was pressed against Nath, it felt oddly comfortable and exciting. He had moved to hold on to my lower back, leaving me clueless about what to do with my hands. He bent a bit, leaning over until he pressed his lips against my forehead.

My heart exploded, and I soon pulled away before reaching out for his face. He seemed surprised, but I didn't give him enough time to react any further since I had pulled him into a rough kiss. I wasn't sure what I was doing and felt relief fill me when he moved to run his hand through my hair as he made to take over the kiss.

Nath was kissing me. I was kissing him. I was kissing a man.

Chapter Ten

For the next few days, I stopped by at Nathaniel's place frequently. We would talk, eat, and sometimes kiss. Kissing. Kissing Nathaniel felt great, and every time we did kiss all I wanted was more. His lips were full and soft, and the moist feeling of his tongue made my heart pound. There was something about his body too that made me want to larch on to him for minutes at a time. He was warm, broad, and it often felt like I was being engulfed.

It's not something I can really explain, but all I can say is that it's definitely exciting.

I learned that Nath was a good cook from his cooking, and I did notice that he prayed. Well, no full-blown well thought out prayers, but small brief mumblings under his breath when he was facing a challenge or the other. The dog he often gave a treat on the street came around from time to time, and Nath gave it food, petting the dog, and sometimes even letting it into the house.

At some point during one of my visits, I had wandered into his bedroom. It was a small plain place with a bed, a study desk, and of course, a bedside table stacked with books. I had sat on the edge, and he had come in looking for me a few minutes afterward. He had sat beside me as I flipped through the books on his desk.

"You read a lot of..." I had trailed, not really sure what religious books and manuals were called.

"Theology," he had answered, leaning back until he was lying on his back on his bed. "I like reading about religion," I had heard him say, making me turn back to look down at him. Nath was tall, really tall. Not Sam's lean lanky tall, but the broad huge kind. I'm not sure if that's a good descriptor. I keep mentioning his height, but it was really fascinating to me as someone almost a whole foot shorter than him.

"Then how come you're not religious?" I had asked him, and a smile formed on his lips as he smiled.

"Learning a lot about religion is the reason I'm not religious," he said. I wasn't exactly sure what he meant by that, but I didn't ask him about it.

Another thing that was memorable about my time with him was once, I had wanted to lie next to him on his bed, so I had gotten out of my clothes — well, not everything. He had burst into laughter at the sight of my underwear, and in his own words: "What the fuck is that?" I hadn't been sure whether to be embarrassed or whether to laugh along with him, because, yes, my temple garments did look confusing.

I think it was that night I decided to stop wearing them. I was committing sacrilege at this point, and the garments themselves clearly weren't keeping me safe from the pollutions of this world. In fact, I had jumped with both legs into the river of sin, and so far, I wasn't regretting it.

A sigh left my lips as I looked down at the journal I had brought down with me. I was scribbling my thoughts away, pausing from time to time to read them to myself, wondering if this was really me.

Am I gay?

The words I had scribbled down in a slanted cursive stared up at me. Well, am I? I kind of repeated to myself, as if wanting an answer from someone. No one was in the room with me, and I'd be damned if I actually asked anyone upright. I could ask Nathaniel, but he would probably roll his eyes and shake his head. I wanted to google it, but servers and their history were monitored.

What does it mean to be gay?

I know it means you like men, but do I like men, or do I just like Nathaniel?

Does this mean I have to give up God?

For a moment I paused writing and stared down at the last point. Did being gay mean that I had to give up God? It was kind of a scary thought to have. God has been my life up until this moment. Sure, I was in a limbo where I just acted without feelings attached to it for the past month. I felt numb. I felt like I wasn't allowed to act like I had before I met Nathaniel — I felt like I was tainted somehow — and by all standards of the church, I was. I wondered if that was what happened to Nathaniel, whether he felt like he shouldn't be religious, and not that he wasn't actually religious.

My mouth opened a bit like I wanted to say something out loud to myself, but I stopped and kept scribbling in my journal. The clock in the room ticked in the background as time passed. I had come down here at around two in the afternoon, and I wasn't sure what time it was now. I was so lost in my thoughts that I didn't realize when the door to the room I was in swung open until Olivia's voice started yelling at me.

"Mathew. Mathew!" the sound of Olivia's voice calling me made me blink before looking up at her. She was staring down at me with a frown and a perplexed look on her face. Her red hair was free today, resting on her shoulders, and covering a bit of her round face.

"I've been standing right in front of you for like five minutes yelling your name," she said, folding her hands over her small chest before letting out a sigh. "You've been distracted lately," she added, looking over at the door. We were in one of the many rooms meant for talking and having classes with people interested in converting. I had wandered down here to have some time to myself after lunch, but it seems that Olivia had found me out.

I closed the journal on my lap as subtly as I could so that Olivia wouldn't notice and ask me what it was. My heart was beating, and I calmed down a bit when her gaze on me didn't waver to my lap where my book was sitting on.

"Why are you here?" she asked me, and I just looked down at the carpet, not wanting to stare at her, and after a while of staying silent, I heard her sigh.

"Okay, if you're not going to answer me I might as well leave, just know that everyone's been looking for you," she said. I waited for her to move away, but she didn't. I was still staring at the floor, but I could see her shoes from the corner of my eyes. I eventually looked up, giving her a puzzled gaze. What did she want?

"Mathew," she said as a look I couldn't quite read took form on her face. "Everyone's worried. We know who you've been seeing." My mouth went open, but I closed it, not sure of what to say.

"Maybe you should have Sam follow you when you go and meet Nath. I don't see why you have to go alone," she muttered, looking from side to side as if she was afraid someone would overhear what she was about to say. "You know he's gay, right? He might not be agreeing to see you in good fate. He must want something."

A frown soon formed on my face when Olivia said that. What did she mean? Did she think Nath was trying to coax me into being alone with him so that he could convince me to... what? I'm not sure what's she's getting at? Did she think he was trying to turn me gay? Does that even make sense?

Well, it did in a way if you looked at it from a sin perspective. You have to be tempted in some way to fall into sin. I agreed with that, Nathaniel was pretty tempting.

I coughed, hiding the laugh that had coursed through me at my thoughts. It was the opposite really. I had been the one to make the move. We kiss, but we don't do anything further. Nath was keeping to his word. He wasn't going to make a move on me. If I wanted something I had to ask.

"It's okay," I said, biting my bottom lip. "He has been doing well. I'm just keeping up with him reading the book of Mormon, nothing much. I just want to help him when he has questions," I said, quite impressed with how well I was getting at lying. I should feel bad about it, but I didn't. I watched as Olivia sighed, playing with the baby hairs at her hairline before sighing.

"Fine," she said, and I smiled at her, watching as she left the room. When the door closed behind her I turned back to face the fireplace, letting my mind wander to what Olivia had told me. She told me people knew, but she didn't exactly specify 'who' they were. Maybe it was just a handful of ministries and not the higher-ups.

A sigh escaped my lips as I looked back down at the brown leather-wrapped journal I had on my lap. I opened it up again, scribbling some things into it. After a while I closed it again, checking the time on my watch. I was past six in the evening, and I had to follow Sam to a house to talk to someone at seven. I got up with my book and pen in hand before leaving the room.

I had no plans of distancing myself from Nathaniel, but I had to be more careful about it. I didn't need people bothering me or getting worried on my behalf.

When I got upstairs Sam was already dressed so I had to change quickly. He didn't say anything out of the ordinary to me which either meant he didn't know Olivia had come down to look for me, or he wasn't the one that told Olivia about Nath being gay. My mind was starting to fuzz over when I tried to think hard about it. How did Olivia know? Did Nath tell her? That's likely, it's not like he was keeping it a secret or anything.

When I was done getting dressed I headed downstairs with Sam, trying not to let the little stray fact bother me. I'll just be more careful from now on.

Chapter Eleven

"So, you've been living on your own ever since you left your mum's place?" I asked, and Nathaniel just nodded as he filled a page of the book in his hand. We were on his bed, lying side by side on our backs. I wasn't really don't anything but watching Nathaniel read. I liked to watch him do just about anything.

I hummed, thinking about what he's been through. To think he started living by himself when he was seventeen and was now twenty-four. I was almost nineteen and I was still a mama's boy. I'm not sure what fascinated me more; the fact that he started living on his own at such a young age, or the fact that he just shrugged it off like it was just another fact of his life.

"Do you miss your mother?" I asked, and I watched as he bit his bottom lip before closing the hardcover book in his hands and putting it away.

"Sometimes," he said, turning to his side so that he could look at me. "But mostly, I'm kind of happy she's getting to sort her life out. I should never have been in it," he said, and I frowned a bit, wondering what he meant by the last part of his statement.

"I should never have been in it."

"You're overthinking things again," I heard him laughed, and I blinked, realizing that I had zoned out yet again. "If you have questions, ask. I'll answer the ones I can," he said, reaching out to run a hand through my hair. He's been doing that a lot lately — touching my hair that is. I wanted to touch his, but I hadn't really gone about touching anywhere beyond his face.

I stared into his dark eyes for a bit, wondering if I should ask him what I was bouncing about in my head. After giving it some thought, I decided to go ahead and ask him. "What do you mean by you never should have been in it?" I asked, and he smiled at me like he had been expecting me to ask just that.

"Well," he started, using his free hand to adjust the pillow under his head. "I'm an illegitimate baby," he laughed, and I just stared blankly at him. "Someone forced himself on my mother on her way back from school and that's how I came to be," he said. The room went silent. I wasn't sure what to say or how to react to that. The fan blades moved slowly creating a low creaking noise. I didn't say anything, and Nath stayed quiet too. He sighed, catching my attention again.

"I don't know where he is." Nath's words when talking about his father a while back suddenly made sense. He didn't just know who he was.

"Well, at least she had you. Aren't you happy to be alive?" I asked, ending the tense silence. I watched on as he chuckled, shaking his head before pulling his hand away from my hair.

"No, not really," he said, turning until he was lying on his back again. "I don't especially think I'm happy to be alive. She should have aborted me. She was only seventeen and afraid."

"She had me because she felt like she was obligated to, not because she wanted to. Christian and all that moral code rubbish," he said with his eyes still on the ceiling above. "And look how I turned out. I'm probably a Christian mother's worst nightmare," he laughed.

"I don't understand. You said she was Christian? As in, past tense?" I asked, and I watched him cock his head as he hummed in response.

"Yeah, my coming out was like the last chip at her faith. Oh well," he said with a chuckle, whistling a bit. The awkward silence returned, and I just stared at him before looking up at the ceiling. It was an old one. You could tell from the tin design you didn't see in houses very often anymore.

My mind was itching with a question, so I eventually gave in and turned to look at Nathaniel. "Then if she's no longer religious why did she kick you out?"

"If someone that looked exactly like the person that did that to you was living under the same roof with you, what would you do?" he asked, and I just looked away, not really sure how to answer his question.

"Exactly," he said, taking my silence as an indication that I agreed with his mother's choice. "Plus, I'm not that selfish. She pretended to love me for seventeen years, I'm glad she gets to reclaim that lost time."

"But you should be happy you exist, though. I'm sure a lot of people are happy you're alive," I said as he turned over to look at me. By people, I meant me, but he didn't need to know about that.

I watched as he sighed, moving closer to me before pressing a kiss to my lips. I closed my eyes, moving my lips against his full ones as he reached out to run a hand through my hair. His lips were soft — they were always soft. And the way he licked my lips made my toes curl. The first few times we kissed I would just stay still or try to mimic his movement without much success, but I could say I was getting a hang of it now. I don't know, hearing him make that low noise that meant he was enjoying himself made me happy.

We kissed for a while until he pulled away from me, humming a bit as he traced the shape of my jaw.

"That's not how it works, Nath. No one misses what they didn't know existed," he said before closing his eyes. I took that as an indication that our discussion was over. He went to sleep, and I laid beside him until it was time for me to leave.

□□□□□□□□

I was reading one of Nathaniel's books on my bed when I heard the door to the room I shared with Sam swing open. Sam walked in, and he gave me a small wave as he headed over to his bed.

"You look excited," I said, sitting up on my bed as I watched him drop his bag and look through his drawers. "What happened?"

"A few people are getting baptized tomorrow," he said, and I just cocked my head to the side. "Isn't that great?" he asked me, and I blinked, realizing that I had zoned out again. I muttered an apology under my breath, before nodding. Sam's smile widened, and he went on to talk about how happy he was not to have lost those people. Most times people agreed to meet with us, then after a few meetings, they just stopped picking our call or outright told us that they were no longer interested.

"What are you reading?" Sam suddenly asked me, making me look down at the book in my hand before closing it and putting it aside.

"Nothing important," I said, placing my hands beside either side of me on the bed. Sam rose a brow at me, but he turned, not questioning me any further. I sighed in relief, looking away from him as well. I was reading a book titled Rediscovering Catholicism. It had been hanging around in Nath's study and I asked him if I could borrow it and he agreed.

As someone who had lived in a tiny Mormon town his entire life the book was fascinating to me It's content familiar yet foreign. I had never known how different denominations could be from each other, and it was interesting to read about how another denomination practiced Christianity.

"Mathew."

"Hmm?" I asked, looking back at Sam's corner of the room. He was giving me an odd look that I couldn't quite tell what it meant.

"How are things with Nathaniel going? Is he willing to have some discussions with us now?" Sam asked, and I bit my lip, shaking my head.

"I'm afraid not," I answered, playing with my fingers. "But he is reading and asking me questions."

The frown that had started forming on Sam's acne filled forehead faded and he smiled instead. The lie had been effortless, but I knew that sooner or later I would have to come up with something else. I couldn't say he was doing that forever.

"Some people are just harder to get to, don't let his lack of progress discourage you," Sam said, going into his pep speech mode. "As long as he's still willing to meet with you, I think you should do it. Olivia was saying it's a lost cause, but if he's still reaching out to you that means he must be interested, right?" Sam said, looking over at me. I nodded, not trusting my mouth to say something that wouldn't give me away.

The fact that I wasn't really doing what I was supposed to be doing hadn't hit me this hard until now. I was kissing and touching the man I was supposed to be preaching to about not doing those exact things with other men, and with women unless he was married to one.

How nice.

After some time, Sam left the room, leaving me alone in the small space. It was well into the evening now, and the street lights were on. I got up from my bed, heading to stand by my window to look out of it. I smiled when I saw Nathaniel walking past with the stray dog that often stuck around him. He was in a white tank top and faded blue jeans. I smiled, watching as Nath and the dog walked out of sight.

I eventually left the window area and headed for my study desk, pulling out my journal before I started scribbling my thoughts on it again. It made me calm, and I felt less overwhelmed when I could see the words instead of having them move around in my head. I had started writing things about the future, and of course, there were a lot of question marks everywhere.

What happens when I come out?

If I come out.

Should I do it soon or wait out my two-year missionary service?

Will I change before then?

I frowned a bit at the words, using my hand to hold up my cheek as I used the pen in my hand to drum against the wooden desk. I couldn't help noticing that I was writing like I had options outside the church. If I got excommunicated, and if my parents kicked me out, where would I go? I tried to stop envisioning Nathaniel as my go to. It's not like he would just let me into his house if something like that happened.

For me, this whole experience was new. It was special. Nathaniel had become the center of my universe very quickly. I adored him, and I'm sure he knew I did but did he feel the same way? probably not. He'd talked to me about past lovers, and he still visited bars around from time to time. I knew I wanted to be with Nathaniel, but did Nathaniel want to be with me?

I knew I wasn't the only one, and I guess I was fine with it. I felt less pressured to commit to something I couldn't promise, and I got to 'experiment' without a fear of attachment.

But I was already attached if I had to be honest with myself. If I pulled back now, it would because I'm a coward and nothing more.

Chapter Twelve

It had rained yesterday so the sky was filled with clouds, and it was a little darker than normal this morning. It was six am, and I was taking a walk with Nathaniel. The brown stray dog was following us, sticking close to Nath, and giving him excited looks. I smiled to myself, chuckling as we made it through the path to the clearing by the lake.

"We come here every day," I said, moving closer to Nath as he shrugged at my statement. We stood next to each other in silence, listening to the frogs croaking, and the sound of the dog lapping at the water.

"It's a habit," Nathaniel suddenly said, making me blink before looking over at him with a curious gaze. "Coming here is a habit," he clarified, fishing for something in his pocket. I watched him pull out a cigarette and a lighter, and soon he was taking a draw. I knew Nath smoked. He did it quite often, but it seemed to be connected to stress so I didn't pry into his business much. I didn't like the smell, and I wondered how anyone could tolerate having that so close to them — in their mouth for that matter.

Maybe it was one of those things Nath told me 'I wouldn't understand' because of my upbringing. That didn't make it any less senseless though.

"Enough about things, how are things on your end," he said, turning to look at me. I hummed, looking away from him. A lot had happened really. Some people had been baptized, I got my first phone call of the year, so I could hear my sisters talk from the other end. I was soon smiling to myself and only snapped out of my thoughts when Nathaniel let out a low laugh.

"Having the time of your life?" he asked, and I just laughed in response, not knowing how to answer that.

He leaned closer to me, and soon his hand was holding on to my head and his lips had met mine. I moved my lips against his own and we were soon kissing each other deeply. His hand moved to tug at the end of my top, but I didn't move. I was excited, hoping for more, but he soon pulled his hand away, and let it rest on my waist.

The water moved by slowly in the lake and the dog that had tagged along started whining. Nathaniel pulled away from the kiss, and we both stared at each other with small smiles until Nath eventually let me go and looked away. He walked to the other end of the cleared area, making me feel a bit sad at the created distance.

"You seem so carefree. Usually, at this point someone in your position would be panicking," he said, chuckling a bit. "Aren't you worried someone will find out, anyone?" he asked, turning back to look at me.

"I am worried," I answered honestly, "but..." I trailed before letting out a low sigh. I bit my bottom lip nervously, wondering what to say. My mind was filled with jumbled thoughts I couldn't quite put into words.

But what? I wondered to myself. I wasn't sure of the future, and I didn't want to think about it. With the way things were going now I might just finish my service and go home, and that would be the end of everything. I was sure even if that happened that Nathaniel would be on my mind.

I wanted to be with him, but I wasn't sure how to make that happen or whether Nathaniel himself would be okay with that.

And then again there was also my church, my friends, and my family. What happens then? I knew I wouldn't just shrug my shoulders like Nath and carry on with my life. I might be aloof, but I wasn't that strong-minded not to feel a sting if people abandoned me.

"What do you want me to do?" I ended up asking. It seemed like I shocked Nath because his eyes went wide, and he almost lost his grip on his cigarette. He looked away from me, putting his cigarette between his lips before letting out a stream of smoke.

"Do what you want," he said, looking down at his shoes. A frown formed on his face like he was irritated, but I knew that wasn't it. "It's your life. Why are you asking me?"

You mean a lot to me, Nath. I said in my head, wanting to say it out loud but I couldn't bring myself to do that. I didn't want to come off as too strong. I had asked Nath why he didn't often 'mess around' with people in the closet and he went on a rant about them being too clingy and indecisive. He had given me a smile right after, telling me I obviously wasn't like that, but it had made me a bit cautious. There were so many mistakes I could make. Just so many of them.

The areas went quiet and none of us said anything for a while. I stared at the blue-green waters of the artificial lake, humming to myself as I thought of what to do. Nath didn't seem like he wanted to answer me, but I needed his answers. I had to know if he saw me the way I saw him.

"Nath?"

"Hmm?" he replied, turning to face me. His frown had disappeared, and he had a dull unreadable look on his face now.

"What do you want me to do?" I repeated, and he just looked away from me. "I'm serious. I have something in mind, but it won't be practical if you don't feel the same way. So, what do you want me to do?" I asked again. It seemed like I had caught his attention this time because he turned to look at me. His dark eyes looked confused. He opened his mouth like he was about to say something, then he closed it shaking his head before looking away.

"I don't want to scare you," he simply said, and I just let out a sigh, looking up at the cloudy sky as I thought about what he said. "I don't want to scare you." His words bounced about in my head, but I would be damned if I knew what he meant even a little bit.

"My sister's part of the church choir now," I said, making Nathaniel turn to me with a confused look. "You said you wanted to know how things were at my end, didn't you?" I asked, and he just smiled, nodding a bit. His hair was in cornrows today, and they looked nice on him, bringing out the shape of his face.

"So, that's a big deal?" he asked.

"Well, yes. I thought you would know since you went to church as a kid." I kicked a stone into the pond and I watched it fly across the air before landing with a loud 'plop.' The dog that had followed up stood up, barking at the water and making Nathaniel laugh.

"Catholics and Mormons are very different," he simply said, and I shrugged. Thinking of the book I had borrowed from him.

"How different?" I asked, making him bite his bottom lip before moving closer to me. We were standing side by side now, and I had to look up at his face.

"For one thing Catholics believe in the Trinity and Mormons don't," Nath started. I could see he was interested in talking about this. Theology was something he really liked discussing and reading about. "Catholics believe in hell, and Mormon's don't," he continued. "Mormons believe people can become Gods, and Catholics don't. Should I go on?" he asked, chuckling as I shook my head and came out of my thoughts. This was becoming an expected outcome. Nathaniel started talking, and I just stared at him until he started laughing.

I watched as Nathaniel looked away, kicking a stone back into the lake. "Shouldn't you be heading back soon?" he asked, making me open my mouth, letting out an oh as I raised my hand to look at my watch.

"I still have a few minutes," I said, tucking my hands back into my pockets as he laughed again.

"You're special," he laughed. I watched him kick another rock into the water. The dog had moved to sit right beside his feet now. If I didn't know any better, I would say the thing was in love with him.

"I like spending time with you," I said out of the blue. Nath turned to me at that, giving me a small smile before looking away. The area went silent again and we just stood there, side by side watching the lake.

"I like spending time with you too." I'm not sure why his words made me flustered, but they did. I looked up from the water to find him looking at me with a small smile. "You're nice to be around."

"Ah," I simply muttered, running a hand through my hair as I looked down at my running shoes. I was wearing my usual jogging pants with a sweatshirt, and of course, Nath was in one of his tank tops and a pair of jeans.

"Mathew."

"What?" I asked, looking back at him. His lips had turned down in a small frown. I watched him let out a sigh. He dropped his cig on the floor, crushing the burning end with his shoe.

"If I fall in love with you I'm sorry," he simply said. I didn't answer him. I just looked away. My face was red, and my heart was beating. This was what I wanted, and I had it, but why couldn't I just tell him that was the case? Why was I just standing in my corner and not doing anything?

When the time came we walked back to the point where we usually met up and I left him behind, still not telling him how I felt about what he had said.

When I got back to the station I slipped into my room as quietly as possible. Sam hadn't woken up yet, so I sat by my study desk and pulled out my journal and began to write my thoughts like I usually did.

Nathaniel apologized to me in advance.

He said he might fall in love with me.

I want that to happen.

Will I ever come out?

I want to be with Nathaniel, but should I be with Nathaniel?

A sigh left my lips when I looked down at those words.

I was a coward.

A selfish one at that.

Chapter Thirteen

"**M**athew." I turned at the sound of my name that had been called over the noisy crowd. I was surprised to find a counselor smiling at me. He was a man with greying hair and tired looking eyes. I stopped in my tracks, pointing at myself, and he nodded. I walked over to him, wondering why he had called out to me.

"Yes, sir?"

Church service had just ended, and the halls were a bit rowdy as people left for their rooms or to the activity rooms. I had to talk to someone later today with Sam and another brother.

"I heard you've been meeting up with the town's local mechanic. Nathan, was it?" I felt my blood drain out of my face at his words. So, people knew. I nodded, and I watched as his lips thinned out.

"Alone?" he asked, and I nodded again.

"Stop meeting up with him," the man said, before reaching out to hold my shoulder. "It's for your own good. If you must, take someone along with you." The smile he gave me afterward didn't seem friendly, and I was left standing in the middle of the hallway when he walked past me. I bit my bottom lip, letting out a sigh before I turned and headed in the direction of our wards. I met up with Sam upstairs and got ready. He went on about a book he was reading, and I listened to him, chiming in to comment from time to time. I was trying to get the counselor's words out of my head. I didn't want to think too much about it.

We headed downstairs to the room, waiting for the person to get there. Sam got up, heading outside for a bit so that he could make a phone call. It took a while, but he came back with the lady that had promised to come. She looked somewhere in her early twenties. She had light brown hair and piercing blue eyes. She apologized for getting here late before taking a seat on the empty sofa.

"Would you like to start off with an opening prayer for us, if you don't mind?" Sam asked her. She looked like she was thinking about it for a bit before she eventually agreed. She said a short prayer, chopped and round about like the type you'd expect from someone who felt it was weird — she probably did, and that was okay. She was learning, and it was fine.

"So, today we're going to talk to you about..." Sam trailed off as he flipped through the little teaching guide. The sound of his action filling the room. "The Word of Wisdom," he said with a smile before placing the book on the table.

"You still have the book we gave you, right?" James, who had come with us for this meeting asked the lady. She blinked, muttering a small 'oh' before fishing for the pamphlet in her bag and flipping to the page we were on.

"So, the Word of Wisdom is a law of health revealed by the Lord for the physical and spiritual benefit of His children," I started, and I watched as the lady nodded in understanding. "The Lord revealed which foods are good for us to eat and which substances are not good for the human body. He also promised health, protection, knowledge, and wisdom to those who obey the Word of Wisdom."

The room went silent for a bit and we all watched as the lady nodded, looking down at the pamphlet in her hands.

"Would you like to read that out?" I asked, and she looked up at me, smiling before she nodded.

"Substances that should not be ingested include; wine, tobacco, strong drinks, and hot drinks," the lady read as she continued to stare down at the pamphlet. She paused, looking up from the pamphlet in her hand to stare at me. "Hot drinks as in? I know strong drinks means something like alcohol."

"Tea and coffee," Sam answered, making her turn to the other end to face him. "You can't drink tea or coffee."

The girl's brows knitted into a small frown as she let out a hum of confusion. "Then how do you stay up if you need to study then? Or something along that like?" she asked, and James moved a bit forward on his seat.

"The Word of Wisdom is to help us with our health. Coffee isn't good for you, and Mormons were given this doctrine long before it was considered a fact by health sciences. This goes to show that heavenly father does love his children and has given us rules like this that will help us."

The lady just stared at James, not really saying anything. My mind wandered a bit far, thinking to Nathan. He smoked like he was a chimney, and he did drink a lot of coffee. He had offered me some while I was at his place and had just sighed and apologized when I rejected his offer.

"Can you continue reading the bullet points, or can I take over?" Sam asked, making the girl look over at him before saying she would do it, and he shouldn't worry. I snapped out of my thoughts, adjusting on my seat before looking over at her.

"The beasts of the field, and the fowls of heaven, and all wild animals that run or creep on the earth may be used as food sparingly and with thanksgiving," she read, before closing the pamphlet.

"Do you understand that?" I asked, and she chuckled.

"Yeah, I get it. You should eat meat in moderation, right?" she said, and we nodded. We watched her cross her feet. She was in lose baggy trousers. "Woah, that's going to be hard. I love me some chicken," she said, making everyone else in the room laugh.

We continued the discussion, and eventually, things came to end after a short prayer led by Sam.

"Have you prayed and asked heavenly father if the words we are telling you are true?" Sam asked, and the girl gave him a small smile as she stood up from the sofa she had been sitting in. The rooms had a homey design to them with comfortable sofas arranged around a small center table. The walls were also decorated with paintings from the scriptures, and there was an electronic fireplace that added to the aesthetic.

"I'm still thinking about it," she said, picking up her handbag.

"Don't take our words for it. You should pray for an answer," James said. She replied with a small 'gotcha' before making to walk over to the room's exit.

"Have you considered coming to service on Sunday?" Sam asked as the girl paused by the door with her hand on the knob.

"I go to my church too, the service times conflict," she said, and Sam just smiled, not saying anything in response. We waved her off, and when she was gone we started to talk to each other. Eventually, James excused himself, leaving me and Samuel behind.

As we started to pack up I heard Sam call my name, making me look over at him. He was arranging the pieces of paper and pamphlets we had used on the center table.

"Did the counselor talk to you earlier?" he asked, and my eyes went wide.

Did he tell him?

"Yes," I answered, frowning a bit. "Did you tell him I was meeting up with Nathaniel?"

"Yeah," Sam said, telling me the truth as he stood up straight. He was looking straight at me with an intensity that made me uncomfortable. "At first, I was all for it, but now I'm a bit worried. I'm starting to think Olivia was right," he said, and I looked down at my shoes.

"What's going on between the two of you?" The question made a lump form in my throat from shock. I opened my mouth, but nothing came out, so I closed it again before running my fingers through my hair in nervousness.

"Something is happening, right? I'm right, am I not?" Sam asked his questions in succession like he was trying to get me to break down and talk to him. When I didn't give in he just let out a sigh, disrupting the silence that had clouded the room during his pause.

"If you need to meet him, I'll follow you, okay?" he said, and I kept looking down at the floor, unable to meet his gaze. I could feel the panic in my chest building up. I didn't want to stop meeting up with Nath — I definitely didn't, and I probably would keep doing it. I nodded at Sam's statement anyway, and I looked up to find him smiling at me. He walked over to me, giving my shoulder a firm grip.

"Stay away from temptation, Mathew," he said, making me blink. "I don't know exactly what is happening, but I can guess. Leave the big fish to people more spiritually grounded. If you're prone to corruption, protect yourself," he said. He was giving me a lecture now and I felt like a little child under his grip and firm look.

"I'll pray for you." And with those words, he walked past me. I listened to his steps as he walked towards the exit. I heard the sound of the door being pulled open, and I heard it close behind him. I let out the breath I had been holding while he was inside with me, and I started fumbling with my fingers, not knowing what to do now.

I left the room after some time, walking past a group of brothers and sisters and not even stopping to say hello. I started wondering how many people knew. Was it just Olivia, Sam and our station's counselor? Did more people know?

When I got to the room I shared with Sam I went straight to my bed, pulling out my phone. I stared at Nath's contact for a while, thinking deeply about it before I eventually went ahead to text him. I had gotten his number a while ago, but I had never actually thought to contact him.

Message to: Nathaniel.

Nath, are you there?

SUN, 7:45 PM.

I stared down at it, wondering how long it would take him to reply. Maybe an hour or so? My eyes went wide when the sound that I had a notification came through. I looked down at my screen, seeing that Nathaniel had replied to my message.

Message from: Nathaniel.

Yes. Is something wrong?

SUN, 7:47 PM.

I bit my bottom lip, deciding to answer him honestly.

Message to: Nathaniel.

Yes. Some people figured it out.

I'm not sure what to do. I don't want to stop seeing you.

SUN, 7: 48 PM.

I saw the three dots pop up, meaning that he was typing, so I sat on my bed, looking down at my screen as I waited for him to send his message.

Message from: Nathaniel.

No more morning walks. No more visiting me at the repair shop. If you need to see me, tell me and I will help you out.

Stay safe, don't be careless.

SUN, 7:50 PM.

I stared down at the text with a mixture of confusion and relief. I was glad he understood, but I had expected...? A more emotional response? A voice in my mind said, filling in the blank. I shook my head, trying to get the disappointment out of my system. Nathaniel knew what he was doing.

Message to: Nathaniel.

Thank you.

SUN, 7:52 PM.

I sent, and soon enough Nath was typing up a response to me again.

Message from: Nathaniel.

No problem.

Also, delete this conversation.

Be careful, okay? I can't stress this enough.

SUN, 7:54 PM.

Message to: Nathaniel.

Okay.

SUN, 7:55 PM.

And with that, the conversation came to an end. I did what he said and deleted the messages. I took a shower and went over to my bed afterward. Laying down on my stomach before closing my eyes as I tried to calm myself. My mind was blowing things out of proportion. That I knew, but I couldn't help it.

Sam got to the room a few minutes later, and after a while, of him moving about he turned the lights off and headed to bed.

I couldn't sleep.

My eyes were wide open as I kept overthinking things. The sound of owls hooting coming from outside didn't help things. I sighed, bringing my cupped palms to my face and did something I hadn't done sincerely in a while.

I prayed.

Chapter Fourteen

- -

After I talked to Nathaniel through text that day, I haven't seen him in person ever since. We talked through the phone from time to time, and I deleted the logs like he told me to. Things seemed to shift back to normal Sam wasn't looking over my shoulder at every opportunity anymore, and Olivia's worried looks had vanished, and she was now her typical bouncy self around me again.

Everything had gone back to normal, except me. I started looking at everyone differently. I was nervous. Would you throw me under the bus if you knew? Was what ran through my mind when socializing with church members for over five minutes at a time.

"It's a bit exhausting."

"It'll pass," Nath said from the other end, making me bite my bottom lip as I stared up at the ceiling. I was in the room that I shared with Sam, not doing anything in particular. It was midday on Thursday, and most people had gone out to knock at doors while I stayed on my bed and thought to myself.

"How have you been?" I asked Nath, sitting up on my bed before laying with the material of the green bedsheet. I heard Nath hum from the other end. I could hear barking in the distance and the turning of screws. He was probably at his workplace. I hoped I wasn't bothering him by calling him up so suddenly.

"I'm doing fine," I heard him say as the sound of something being lifted followed. "I miss you though," he added in a soft voice like he wasn't quite sure he was supposed to say that. A smile made its way to my lips, and my chest felt full.

"I miss you too," I said into the phone, and Nathaniel stayed quiet on the other end. After a long pause, Nath finally spoke up.

"How are things at home?" he asked. My lips when thin. I was a bit disappointed he was trying to change the topic, but I didn't bother and just answered his question.

"Things are fine. I've been emailing my parents back and forth," I answered, and I heard him hum from the other end. "My sisters say they miss me since they actually have to do chores now," I added, and Nathaniel laughed. I smiled as I thought about them.

"Do you have any siblings?" I asked.

"No, it was just me and my mum," he said, and I heard a huff afterward. He had probably moved something. "I'm used to being by myself."

I didn't know what to make of that, so I just stayed silent on my end.

"Though, there was this traditional Baptist woman with nine kids on my street, lord," he said with a little chuckle, and I laughed too.

"How's your relationship with your siblings. I'm always curious how people live so many people in the same house," he said, and I smiled.

"Well, my family house is pretty big."

"Oh really?" he asked with a sarcastic tone and I laughed, getting up from my bed. I wondered over to the window, looking out as I hummed to myself. People should start heading back sooner or later if I was correct.

"Yeah, but like not extravagant. It's a farmhouse. We have chickens and a little vegetable patch," I said, and Nath hummed from the other end.

"Wow, you had enough space for a garden?"

"Is that weird?" I asked.

"Well, I mean, in the city, yeah," Nath said, and I heard someone calling his name from the side of his line. He shouted something back to them before apologizing to me for the sudden pause.

"It's okay," I said, letting my eyes look onto the road. I smiled when I saw the stray dog walked by. It hadn't rained in a while, so the red clear grounds were dry and cracked.

"So, more about our childhoods," he said, making me laugh.

"I went to church three times a week. On Wednesdays for stations of the cross, on Fridays for the 'A Day With the Lord' program my mother was obsessed with, and Sundays — well, that's universal," he said, chuckling.

"My case was somewhat similar. We went for a lot of weekday church activities," I said, running my hand through my hair as I bit my bottom lip. I was still looking out the window, not really sure of what to focus my gaze on. "Did you like going to church?" I asked after a while of both of us not saying anything.

"Yes," he answered, and I heard the sound of metal moving. He was probably looking through a toolkit. "The thing is, it just felt comforting? Like a habit? It's not like I'm actually Christian. I still pray sometimes. I still visit the Catholic church in the other town," he went on, and I listen to him.

"Do you ever feel that way?" he asked, making me blink back. "Do you ever feel like going to church is just a hobby to you?"

"No," I answered, and I heard Nath sigh from the other end. I could tell he was rolling his eyes. He always did that when I said something, and he thought I was being dishonest.

"Seriously Mathew, think about it. You grew up Christian, most of your fun activities have an attachment to church in some way or the other. Sure, the church is part of your person. It's all you've ever known. It might not necessarily be part of your belief. Do you ever feel like you're doing certain things like praying just because?" he asked, I leaned away from the window sill, licking my lips as I went to sit on my bed again.

"It's not like that." My voice shook, and I was gripping my bedsheet. Why was I acting like this? That wasn't the case at all. If anyone was delusional about their beliefs it was Nath.

"What about you? Are you sure you believe you're not religious because you think you shouldn't be? You're gay, and you think you shouldn't..." My words were coming out badly worded. I couldn't really find a good way to phrase them.

"What do you mean by I'm gay? We both know that. You're gay too," he said in an irritated tone before pausing. "Unless you don't think that's the case."

I didn't answer him. I stayed quiet and he just sighed, not saying anything for a while.

"I won't bother talking about, and back to your question. No, some things don't mix. Gay or Catholic. I had to pick one—"

"You didn't have to," I cut in and he groaned. He sounded angry, and I wasn't just sure why I couldn't just shut up and listen to him. Maybe I was afraid he would say something that would confuse me.

"Look. I'm not going to convince myself that I can be the two at the same time. I don't care what other LGBT+ people have convinced themselves into thinking. That's their business, it's not my life, but to me, it seems illogical to grasp onto something that has no regard for your person," he said. "Think of it this way. If you come out to your church members and decide that yeah, you still want to be Mormon, that you still want to go to church and all that gaze. I can list a bunch of things that will happen."

There was brief silence on the other end, and soon Nath started talking. "You won't be able to enter a temple, and you might be excommunicated if you don't follow their silly; yeah you can be same-sex attracted, and Christian. Just marry a woman and not actually do anything a gay person would do, like sleep with men, okay?" he said the last part in such a condensing tone that it hurt.

"Be honest with yourself Mathew," he added after a while of silence.

"Look, I can sit here and listen to you go on and on about things you don't understand..." I trailed in a shaking voice. I was shaking.

"I understand Mathew, I grew up similarly. In a very religious household, and—"

"I'm Christian, Nath, stop this. You're starting to sound like all those 'preachy' missionaries you're always complaining about." My voice was firm now, and Nathaniel didn't say anything back to me. I could hear him breathing on the other end. My breathing was heavy too, and my mind was buzzing with unease.

"You know what? I'll call you later. Take care Math," he said into the line before hanging up. I sat down with the beeping noise from my phone ringing through my eyes for a while before I eventually put my phone down. I had never fought with Nath, and it was making me uneasy. Should I text him now? Should I wait for tomorrow to text him back?

I had paced about my room and crawled under the covers of my bed when I heard my phone vibrate with a notification. I reached out to the bedside table, picking up my phone before looking to find a message from Nath.

Message from: Nathaniel.

You're right, and I'm wrong. I'm sorry for even bringing that up.

FRI, 7: 30 PM.

I stared down at the text, not really knowing what to make of it. It looked like he didn't mean it, and he had just sent it to me to be the bigger person.

That only made me more irritated.

Message to: Nathaniel.

Stop being condescending.

FRI, 7:32 PM.

I sent, and the dots showing that he was texting me back soon popped up.

Message from: Nathaniel.

I'm trying, and I'm sorry. It's a sensitive topic. I get it. You're having a hard time, and cornering you like that was rude. It's just sometimes... I'm sorry.

FRI, 7:33 PM.

Looking down at the text I bit my bottom lip before letting out a sigh. I didn't know how to reply to that, so I just changed the topic. I didn't want to be angry at Nath.

Message to: Nathaniel.

We should meet up sometime. We haven't seen each other in a while.

FRI, 7:34 PM.

He replied with a smiley face, and I wasn't sure how to respond, so I didn't. I took that as the end of the conversation. We both needed time to cool off anyway. After a while, Samuel opened the door to the room we shared and walked in. He chatted with me through the time he went about doing his business. That night I couldn't sleep. Nathaniel's words were swimming in my head, and they made me uncomfortable — a little scared.

Chapter Fifteen

- -

Since the argument I had with Nath, we haven't really spoken much to each other. We would text each other vague things from time to time, then whatever conversation started would be lost in about three or so back and forth sentences. I wondered if he was angry with me, or if he just thought I needed space the think. The worry made me a little dysfunctional. I kept zoning out of consciousness, and people would have to touch or yell at me to grab my attention in crowds or during meetings.

Sam and Olivia's worried gazes had returned. Olivia had even pulled me aside and asked me to talk to her, but I had just shaken my head and slipped past her before she could pull me back. I didn't have time for anyone or anything.

I was in my room writing an email to my mother when I heard my phone vibrate from a call coming in. I looked around, hoping that Sam was nowhere in sight, and when I confirmed that, I checked my phone to find that it was Nathaniel calling me like I had expected. A lump formed in my throat. It's been a few days since things became weird between us, and I wasn't sure if a phone call would change that. I answered the call anyway, staying silent on my end.

"Hello?" he finally asked after a while of me just breathing into the line.

"Hi." My response was low and unenthusiastic, but my heart was racing. I had missed his voice. So much.

"How have you been?" he asked me, and I bit my bottom lip. I could hear some of the background noise from his end. It sounded like he was in the kitchen because I could hear the sound of cutlery clicking, as well as the sound of something sizzling.

"I've been doing fine," I answered, running my tongue over my dry lips. "You?" I added, desperate for the conversation not to evaporate into thin air.

"I've been busy," he simply said, and I muttered a small 'oh.' Busy. Yes, I should have expected that. He did work back to back and across two towns.

"I went over to the next town the day before yesterday and spent some time at a friend's place." A friend. I repeated in my head as my lips drew into a thin line on my face. I shouldn't be getting jealous. I knew that. It's not like we were dating, and said friend could actually be just a friend, but my thoughts loved being illogical and making me worry for no reason. It's just that I've seen him flirt around, and it hurt.

You're not dating. A voice said in my head and my felt my face warm up. Yes, we weren't. I shouldn't feel this way at all. All we've done is kiss and talk, and at the end of the day, I might not even have the courage to come out.

"He helped me get out from my brooding state." Nathaniel laughed after that, but I wasn't amused. I just played with my fingers, looking down at them as I waited for the conversation to change. If he was seeing someone

I didn't really want to hear about it but butting in to tell him not to talk about it would be rude.

"I'm really sorry for bringing up what I did that day." My eyes widened as his words reached me. I didn't know what to say to that, so I didn't say anything. I stayed still on my chair, and both ends of the call were silent until Nath continued talking. "I don't know. Maybe I just assumed you would understand things from my perspective, but you're right. We're not the same person. We don't have the same exact experiences, and I don't understand what you're going through as much as I think I do." For some reason, I felt a bit distressed by his words. I wasn't sure why. Maybe it's because I felt like I should be apologizing too, but I didn't really have anything to say.

"Math?" I blinked at the sound of my name, realizing that I had zoned out for a bit and probably missed a bit of what Nathaniel had said.

"Sorry, I — sorry," I muttered, not really knowing how to explain myself. I heard Nath chuckle from the other end.

"It's okay," he said, and an awkward silence followed.

"I said the friend I'm talking about invited me to come over again. I was thinking this weekend. Do you want to come?" he asked me.

A frown made its way to my face as I hummed. Why? So that you can rub it in my face? Of course, I didn't say this out loud. It was jealously speaking, and I was embarrassed about thinking like that. It's not like I could even tell Nath about how I felt because it was petty and illogical. Being around Nath had made me realize I had a potential for jealously I had never even known. I didn't care about most people, but for some reason, I was irritated whenever it involved Nath. I didn't like feeling like this.

"Mathew."

"I'm sorry. I keep zoning out," I apologized, sighing before sitting up in my chair.

"So, do you want to come?" Nathaniel asked me again, and I bit my bottom lip.

"Where exactly are you going, and when?" I asked, and he laughed.

"You really weren't listening to me, were you?" he asked. I could almost see him rolling his eyes. A small smile made its way to my lips as I chuckled. It was my first sincere laugh in a while.

"This weekend, over at the town I work at sometimes. Do you want to come?" he asked, and I thought about it.

"Well, I'm not allowed to be out—"

"I know that. I could sneak you out," he cut it and I rose a brow. "It's not going to be hard."

"Really?" I asked in a teasing tone. Was I teasing Nath? Was I doing that? It seemed like that.

"Yes, really," he said, mimicking my tone. "So, do you want to come?" he asked, and I looked down at my desk. I had brought out my journal sometime before I started writing the mail back home. It was open to a page I had been scribbling on with green ink. The words 'Does Nathaniel hate me now?' stared right at me in bold letters. My computer had gone to sleep, and it was just me in the quiet room.

"Sure," I answered reaching out to close my journal. I heard Nathaniel mutter a 'great' from the other end. After giving him a positive answer, I started to feel a bit nervous. How exactly would he sneak me out? Would anyone notice if I was gone for a whole night — possibly the whole weekend? I started to worry, but the sound of Nath's voice from the other end pulled me out of my thoughts.

"You've been zoning out a lot lately," he commented, and I shrugged, feeling my baby hairs at my hairline with my fingers.

"I know." A breath left my lips and I rested my head on my desk, still holding my phone to my ear as I stared at Sam's corner of the room. It was neat and tidy, and of course, he had a bunch of books and pamphlets sitting at the foot of his bed.

"That means you've been thinking a lot about something, right?" Nath asked, but I didn't respond to him. The other end also went silent soon, and I was just holding my phone to my ear, not saying anything. I didn't have anything to say, and it seemed neither did Nath.

"Are you still angry with me?" he suddenly asked, and I sat up on my chair with wide eyes.

"No," I said firmly, and I heard him sigh from the other end.

"I don't know. It just seems like it, and I feel like I'm bothering you, and you don't really want to talk to me—"

"You're not bothering me," I cut in. At that moment I wished I was with him so that I could see his expression. Nath had a very walk around way when it came to him talking about how he felt, and you could only ever tell how he was really feeling from his expression. He sighed, and his end went quiet for a while.

"Okay. I'm glad. I'll talk to you later," he said, and I smiled. "I'll come and get you on Friday evening, then I'll bring you back before eight in the morning. Does that sound okay?" he asked, and I muttered a small 'yes.' The idea of meeting up with Nathaniel again made my stomach churn with a feeling of happiness. Things would be awkward, but at least I would get to see him.

"I hope you're ready for a road trip," he said, and I chuckled.

"Yeah..." I trailed.

"Okay then, I'll talk to you later." And with that he hung up, leaving me to listen to the string of the beeps that followed. I put my phone away soon after and went ahead to continue writing my email to my mother. I wasn't sure what more to say in it. There was a lot to talk about, but they weren't things I could disclose to them.

To: JiHeePark@gmail.com

Subject: I've been learning a lot recently.

It's been a handful of months since I left home. I thought I was going to be homesick and a little bored here, but things are interesting. Apart from spreading the word and having a closer communion with my brothers and sisters, I've gotten to see life outside a small town. I'm not sure how to describe my experiences. I'll just say it has taught me a lot.

How's everyone doing? I hope the girls don't miss me too much. Ask them to pray for me and tell them I'm doing alright.

I stared at the email for a while before pressing send. It felt empty — It looked empty, but there was nothing I could really do about it. I couldn't really tell them what was going on. A wave of sadness hit me, and I suddenly understood how it must feel for people to hold on to such secrets. It felt like living a lie. No, more like living two lives. The person I was around friends and church members had become a shell of myself due to the things I had to hide from them. I was only a few months into this secret, but it was exhausting.

After saying a short prayer under my breath, I got up from my seat before heading over to sit on the edge of my bed. I didn't want to think about it too much. I wasn't ready to tell anyone. I was still confused. I tried to think of happy things, like having my first real conversation with Nath since our fight, and the fact that I would get to see him this weekend. It worked. I was soon smiling and humming along to one of my favorite hymns; Have I Done Any Good?

Chapter Sixteen

"Are you sure no one will go around looking for you?" Nath asked me as he made a turn. I nodded, looking away from him to stare at the road ahead. Early in the evening, he had come up to the side of my window, surprising me. It took a while, but he climbed up and helped me set things before helping me down. My chest was still swelling from adrenaline and the stupid smile on my face had refused to leave.

We were in a truck-like car with no back seat. Music was playing on the radio and I looked out the window to watch the scenery pass by. The roads were lifeless — empty for the most part. We've been on the road for at least three hours now, and it was starting to get dark.

"Are we heading straight to your friend's place?" I asked, turning to face Nathaniel. His hair was in a low puff today, and he was wearing a proper shirt and a jacket instead of a tank top. He looked like he was dressed up for something, but I couldn't tell what.

"No, we're stopping at a local bar first," he said, making me raise a brow at him. He looked at me before turning back to the road. "I'm not going to make you drink alcohol if that's what you're thinking," he said, and I just hummed.

"I just want you to loosen up a bit. Have fun." I didn't have a reply to that. I wanted to spend time with Nath. That was fun to me, not hanging around in a bar with other people. I clenched and unclenched my fist, trying to calm myself. I didn't want to ruin everything by being moody, so I just decided to trust Nath.

After some time, Nath pulled out of the road and drove into a small clearing by a low building. I looked out of the window, staring at the place that looked dead. Were people even inside? Nath soon unlocked the doors and climbed down. He turned to me, motioning for me to get down too before closing his door. I hesitated, but after a while, I climbed down from the car and closed the door behind.

Nath had already started heading for the building, so I had to do a little jog to catch up to him.

As I walked into the building the music hit me. I felt a bit sick and nauseous. It was dark, but the flashing colorful lights were playing with my vision, and the crowded and noisy area didn't help things at all. I just stood there, not knowing what to do before Nath waded through the crowd and grabbed my hand. He pulled me through the sea of people until we got to an open space around tables. He held on to both my shoulders, helping me into a seat before he took the one beside me.

"Are you okay?" His tone was worried. I felt bad for making him worry.

"I feel fine," I answered as my heart rate went down. I was still squinting at the lights, but my ears were getting used to the noise. "This place is rowdy."

"It always is," Nath said in an offhand comment. I turned to look at him. He was smiling at me, and his brown eyes were giving me a look I really couldn't read. I looked away because of the intensity of his gaze.

"How come they didn't ask for any ID? We just walked in," I said, turning back to him. Nath sighed, covering his face with his hand.

"Do you want anything? Water, juice—"

"Nath."

"They don't care about that here," he said, waving his hand. "Plus, what are you afraid of, you're eighteen aren't you?" he asked, and I nodded. My eyes moved away from him to look into the crowd. They went wide in shock when I realized that it was just men. Men, men, and lots of men. A lump formed in my throat as I watched a pair exchange a kiss on the lips, my hand formed a fist on my lap as I turned back to Nathaniel with a panicked expression on my face.

"Nath."

"Hmm?" he asked, looking up from his phone.

"What kind of bar is this?" I asked, watching as he sighed.

"It's a gay bar, why are you asking?" The blood drained from my face, and I stared down at my lap, not knowing what to say.

"Look, no one knows who you are. They didn't even ask for your ID. Have fun, okay?" he said reaching out to hold my hands. I pulled it away, refusing to give him a reply. I was still shocked, and wary. A gay bar. I thought to myself, looking up from my lap to look around the room. Men dancing together, kissing, and casually holding hands. A gay bar.

What was I doing here?

"Do you want to dance?"

"No." My answer was firmed, laced with — fear? I don't know. All I knew was that I didn't want to be out there with the crowd. Part of the crowd.

"Suit yourself," Nathaniel said as he stood up. I looked over at him, watching as he got up and walked away from the table and into the crowd. I didn't know how to feel, so I just watched him, sitting still in my seat as I watched Nathaniel ease into a conversation like he knew the people. He probably did.

I watched on as he danced with one man to another, shared a drink or a brief hug. my heart was starting to race, and a lump was forming in my throat as I watched him. I couldn't help but feel that he looked more in tune and in place with them. With me, he always got irritated at some point. My lips formed a thin line as I watch someone hold on to him by the waist before laughing.

Why was I still watching him interact with men in the crowd? It was a sadistic thing to do to myself.

I got up, feeling dizzy and nauseous. I started making my way towards the exit, wanting to be out of the bar. I didn't want to watch Nathaniel have fun with others. That's not what I had in mind when he asked me to follow him to his friend's place. I was soon outside in the dimly lit parking lot. My skin was kissed by the cool air and I shivered in response. It took a while for my heart to start beating properly. I was still dazed and recovering from my shock when I heard my name being called. I turned around to find Nath calling out to me with wide eyes as he walked in my direction.

"Why did you leave so suddenly?" he asked me. His voice was loud, and I just looked down at the floor when he stopped right in front of me.

"It's really none of your business." I wasn't sure why I was saying that. Maybe I was angry and frustrated with myself. Maybe I was jealous. Maybe it was all of the above.

"What?" I looked up to find a puzzled look on Nath's face. He looked confused Shrugging my shoulders, I looked down at the ground again.

"Go and dance and drink with them. You seemed to be enjoying yourself."
I looked up. Nath's lips were in a thin line. "You might as well kiss them
too. I know you do. I know I'm not the only one—"

"What are you going on about?" he asked, cutting me off.

I stared at him, opening my mouth them closing it before tucking my
hands into the pockets of my trousers. "I really don't know. I don't know,"
I muttered.

"I came here to have fun with you. You said you didn't want to dance. You
don't drink. Anything beyond kissing makes you uncomfortable. Well,
what do you want? Help me out here because I'm so confused," Nath said
in a pleading tone.

"You're telling me you know you're not the only one. Is that an accusation
of something? We're not dating. You're going to leave here and forget all
about me in a while so why does it seem like you're trying to get some sort
of faithfulness out of me? Are you trying to torture me, or don't you care
about how self-centered you're being? Or do you think you're the only one
with feelings?"

He stopped talking, and I didn't respond to him. The area went quiet and
we just looked at each other. I bit my bottom lip, not knowing what to do.
I'm not sure how it happened but my eyes started to water and soon I was
sobbing. Nath's eyes went wide with shook, and he soon pulled me to his
chest, holding me close as I cried. When I calmed down a bit he pulled me
away, looking down at me with a worried look.

"Are you okay?"

"I don't know," I answered with honesty. I could feel my hands shake, and
my lips were trembling, and I was shivering though it wasn't cold. I blinked
when Nath's hands found their way around my face, cupping it in his
hands before he leaned over to press a kiss to my lips. Once, twice, and soon

I was kissing him back, realizing that I wanted more. His hands had moved to my back, pulling me closer. I didn't know where to put my hands, so I nested them on his chest, sighing into the kiss as it became deeper.

Nath pulled away again, and soon he was kissing my cheeks, the soft spot under my now wet eyes, and my neck. I shivered as his hands moved under my shirt, pressing my skin, molding it lightly like they were desperate to touch something but didn't know what.

"Mathew."

"Hmm?"

"We should stop," his voice was low — unsure. He didn't sound like he wanted to stop, and it seemed like he was banking on me to pull away out of fear. I shook my head, reaching out to pull his face down a bit so to my lips met his again. His lips were soft as usual.

I let out a low stutter when his insistent lips parted my shaking ones. I gave in, still kissing him, still not wanting to run away.

He pulled away after a while, staring down at my face as he ran the base of his thumbs over my cheeks. "You confuse me," he said as his brown eyes gazed down at me. I cast my gaze to the ground, feeling overwhelmed.

"I'm s-sorry," I muttered, not knowing what to say. I was confused too. I heard Nathaniel sigh, and soon he had pulled away from me completely. I felt little tingles in the area his thumbs had been. I looked up to find him looking down at me with a small smile.

"We should head to my friend's place. It's getting late." I nodded at his words, and we walked over to the truck we had come in, getting in. I sat in the passenger seat in silence as Nath started the car and hummed along to the rap music that started playing. It had been put on pause when he parked.

"I'd rather not live like there isn't a God Than die and find out there really is Think about it."

I wanted to ask Nath what the song was called, and who was the singer because the last few lyrics sounded relatable. I wasn't sure if that was the purpose of the song, but that was how I felt. That was why I was afraid.

Nath soon drove the truck out of the parking lot and into the main road. I watched him from the corner of my eye, happy to see that he didn't seem too fazed by my hissy fit from before.

"We're almost there. Give or take, ten minutes and we'll be at his place," Nath said, and I blinked as I came out of my thoughts.

"Nath," I called out his name and soon he had turned to look at me with a raised brow.

"Sleep with me." I wasn't sure how my request would be answered when I had thought it up in my mind, but I hadn't imagined Nathaniel would laugh at me. He was laughing, making my cheeks grown warm as I wondered why.

"Mathew," he started, shaking his head a bit. "I don't think you'll want that. You'll hate yourself for the rest of your life if you decide that you actually want to be a churchman with a wife, kids, and all that jazz."

"I won't let you do something stupid on a whim," he said, turning away from me to look at the road ahead. "Also, you're doing it again — being selfish. If you sleep with me and you break my heart in the future would you expect me to just shrug it off?"

I bit my bottom lip. I knew what I wanted. I wanted him, but he was right. I was scared, and I might pick the easy route at the end of the day.

We got to the apartment complex a few minutes later, and I followed Nath to the flat his friend lived in. The man was tall, just like Nath and I sat in the corner as I watched them catch up. There were many inside jokes that I really couldn't understand, and of course, I got jealous when the man got too close and their conversation started to seem more like flirting.

But it was fine. I was supposed to be okay with it. We weren't dating, and Nath didn't owe me any explanations.

I really was a small part of Nathaniel's life, but it was okay because I was supposed to be easy to forget when I left. He's already a big part of my life. A lump formed in my throat at the thought. At night I shared the bed in the guest room with Nath. I watched him sleep since I couldn't. He looked a little less intimidating when he slept. I wouldn't say he looked smaller. He looked more like a gentle giant. His features were softer, and the resulting expression was almost childlike.

He was right in front of me. All of him. And I couldn't have him because I was scared and confused. He wanted someone who wouldn't look over their back when with him. Someone who would dance with him in the club without panicking — someone he didn't have to sneak around with.

I wasn't that someone, and it hurt.

Chapter Seventeen

We left at the dawn of the morning. The car was quiet throughout the ride besides the occasional sigh from Nath. I was not sure what he was thinking about, but I decided to let it be.

It wasn't until we drove into town that Nath turned to me. I could see him from the corner of my eyes. His brown eyes were set on me like he was trying to figure something out. I didn't look over at him because of the intensity of his gaze, and the fact that he might notice that my eyes were red and puffy. I might have sobbed last night, and I never got around to sleeping until late in the night.

"I took you out because I wanted us to have fun," he said before he looked away, easing into the dirt roads. "I'm sorry things turned out the way they did."

"It's fine," I muttered. My voice was shaky, and I wasn't sure why it was that way. My mind was buzzing with questions I was asking myself, and a lump wedged itself in my throat anytime I thought of having to end this sooner or later.

I didn't want to.

But I was too much of a coward to set my foot down and take the leap.

I heard Nathaniel sigh at my reply, and the car soon went silent again. He drove all the way to the front of my room's window. We got down, and he helped me climb back into my room, using the concrete footing around the windows as mini stairs. I had checked the time in Nath's car before we got out. It was currently past five in the morning, and I doubt anyone was awake. When I made it into my room I turned around, looking down at Nath. He waved, and I waved back before watching him walk back to his car and driving off.

A small smile made its way to my lips. It wasn't a smile of happiness, more of a smile of confusion and pretense. If only that alone could convince me that everything was okay. After a while of looking out into the roads that were bathed in the blue-yellow color of the early morning, I stepped back from the window, looking behind me to find Sam fast asleep. A small chuckle escaped my lips. I guess I should be grateful for the fact that he slept like a rock. He didn't react to me moving about the room as I freshened up and returned to bed as if I had never left.

Later in the day, I went out with Sam as usual. Knocking on doors, sharing pamphlets and answering questions, but my mind wasn't there. I was thinking of something — someone. I wondered what Nath was doing. I wondered whether he thought of me as much as I thought of him.

"Mathew." I blinked, realizing I had spaced out again. Sam had been talking to me about something, though I can't remember what exactly. We were standing in the middle of the hallway with a handful of other people dotting the corners.

"I'm sorry, what were you saying?" I asked, running my fingers through my dark hair as I looked up at him in embarrassment. His lips drew into an even thinner line. He was losing his patience with me. It was clear from his expression.

A frown formed on Sam's face as he let out a sigh before shaking his head. "I'm worried about you," he said, looking down at the clipboard in his hand before pointing at my name that was written at the top in a nice cursive print.

"Listen. I was talking to you about the service this Sunday. You're supposed to be the one at the pulpit," he said, and I nodded.

"Please don't zone out while giving a sermon. I beg you," he said, and I gave him a tired smile, apologizing again. Sermons. I used to love giving those, but since I arrived here I've been feeling more of like a prop, than an actual person whenever I was chosen to read out passages at the pulpits or give out sermons. My preaching felt more like lips service, than anything that came from the heart. I had also started to dodge partaking in the sacrament, and I was overall not just myself anymore.

"Mathew."

"What?" I blinked, realizing that I had done it again. I had zoned out. "I'm sorry," I muttered immediately afterward, covering my face with a palm before sighing. What is wrong with me?

Sam wasn't giving me a reaction. He just stared at me. I took my hand away from my face, looking at him with a puzzled look. Did he have something to say to me? He had his lecture face on, and I didn't like it.

I watched as his gaze shifted from me to the people talking a few meters away from us. "Can I talk to you in private?" he asked, and I nodded, not trusting my mouth to say anything sensible. He smiled, and he then turned, walking away. I followed him through the hallways, and eventually into one of the many rooms we used to talk to people. Sam took a seat on the closest sofa, and I decided to sit across from him.

We sat in silence. The fan blades above us moved with creaking noises. I could hear my own breathing and heartbeat. My lips felt dry, so I licked them, looking away from Sam to avoid his intense gaze. What does he have to say to me? I wondered, starting to worry if he had figured out I was gone last night. He couldn't have figured that out, right?

I snapped back to reality when the sound of Sam cracking his knuckles made me look up at him.

"I know you're struggling," he said in a calm tone. I rose a brow, wondering what this was about.

"You're acting this way because of Nath, aren't you?" he asked, and my eyes went wide. I wanted to deny it. I wanted to yell 'no' like his suggestion was the most ridiculous thing I had ever heard, but my lips were sealed. I don't know. I just felt — tired.

"So I'm correct?" he went on, but he didn't wait for my answer before he continued talking. "Olivia and I thought you were handling it fine, and I thought you were starting to get back into shape, but I think this is serious." My gaze was on him. I was frozen in place. I didn't know what to do or how to react. He was right. It was serious.

I was in love with Nath. More than in love with him — whatever qualifier that would take.

"We talked yesterday, and..." he trailed, not meeting my eyes. I frowned, wondering what he was too hesitant to say. "We decided to ask if you'd consider counseling. You know. You have to talk to someone, you can't keep it all in—"

"What's the counselor supposed to do?" I asked. My voice was high, loud and firm. Sam seemed taken aback. He blinked, sitting up straight on the sofa with brown cushion material. "What's he going to do, huh? Un-gay me? Is that it?" I asked, my voice even louder. I wasn't sure where I had gotten this courage from, but it was oozing out of me now. Keeping everything inside myself must have done this. I was so done, so done with overthinking everything.

"Mathew—"

"I'm in love with him Sam." Why was I oversharing? I needed someone to talk to. God, I needed to let my thoughts out. They've been behind a cage for so long. "I love him so much, and..." I trailed, looking down at my hands. They were shaking, but my tongue was still desperate to speak. "I want him to love me back. I'm so confused." It seems like my last sentence confused Sam. I wasn't sure what he was expecting me to say, but what I had uttered wasn't it.

He thought it was the other way around. If only. If Nath was madly in love with me like I was with him I wouldn't be this

"He's not pushing you to do this?" Sam asked. My eyes went wide with confusion, and then I frowned.

"No, of course not," I said before looking down at my shoes. They were well polished, so much so that they reflected my face back at me. I sighed, running my fingers through my dark hair before I looked over at Sam. My hair had grown a little longer over the course of the past months. Nath liked it, so I kept it that way.

"Have you—?" Sam's question was suspended in the air like he was trying to find a polite way to say this. "Have you always liked men? Is this something you've been struggling with even before we got here." A frown formed on my face before I shook my head. No. No. It was just Nath and Nath alone. He was the only one I've ever thought of in this way, man or woman.

"I see..." he trailed, and the room went silent. We both sat there, not saying anything to each other. After a while, I looked over at Sam and he raised his gaze to meet my own.

"We're friends Mathew," he said, and I nodded. yes, Sam was my friend. I've known him his kindergarten. "I want to help you," he said right after, and I nodded again, bringing my hands to my face and covering it.

"I'm thinking you should see a counselor—"

"That won't work," I cut it, taking my hands away from my face before shaking my head.

"How do you know that?" Sam asked. "You don't know that," he stated firmly right after.

"Of course, I won't tell anyone without your permission, but you have to get help. You'll be here for another year, and you'll still have to be around him. That's dangerous." I bit my bottom lip as I listened to his words. Even if I left this town and headed back home now, I knew nothing would change. I would still be in love with Nath, and it was a little frustrating that Sam was framing it as being as simple as avoiding it 'problem.'

"What if," I started, pausing. Sam rose a brow at me, wedging his chin on the small padding he created with both his hands. "What if I don't want to do anything about it? What if I'm fine with it?"

Sam stared at me with a calm look, but I could tell he was horrified by my words from the way his eyes fixed on me and the way his nostrils flared.

"You don't really think that," Sam said. It was not a question. It was a statement. He believed I couldn't think that — shouldn't think that, but I did. I really did. I opened my mouth but closed it before letting out a small sigh.

"Do you really want to continue like this? Can't you see how unhappy and unstable it's making you feel?" Sam added, making me stare at him again.

"No." I shook my head, folding my hands over my chest. "It's not that. That's not the reason," I said, looking down at the carpet. "It's the anxiety from hiding things from everyone that's eating at me. Plus, I'm not even sure Nath sees me the way I see him — or maybe he doesn't want to, I'm not sure," I added, and Sam's eyes went wide.

"I want him to love me, Sam," I said. I was heaving. I needed some air. I needed some natural light. No, both. I got up before heading over to the windows that were covered with heavy curtains. I pulled them aside, letting the dim light of the evening flood the room.

"Sorry about that," I said as I turned to look at Sam before walking back to take a seat on the sofa.

"So, you're not going to the counselor?"

"I'm not going to the counselor," I said in a firm tone, and Sam just gazed at me. We stared at each other for a while until Sam eventually stood up from his seat. He adjusted his tie, wedging the clipboard he had been holding under his armpit before he looked down at my sitting figure.

"I can't promise you that I won't tell someone who can help when the time comes," he said. His eyes were cold and void of emotion. "This isn't something you can handle yourself, but I'll let you be for now."

"I'll continue praying for you," he said, and with that he was gone, leaving me in the room by myself.

Chapter Eighteen

I was shaking.

Tapping the microphone in front of me I tried to calm myself before I looked down at my notes. It was Sunday, and I was giving my sermon. Most times I was able to speak through the lump in my throat and my foggy mind, but today my distress felt worse. Regardless, I did finish my sermon and left the podium with a round of applause. The church was a bit more filled up today, we had started getting regulars from the town. I settled down beside Sam, and he didn't turn to look at me.

He's been cold since that day he got me to talk to him, and you could bet I was counting the time I had left until he told more people. Olivia had also been different about me. Asking me to come to her if I needed someone to talk to or pray with. I knew she had full details courtesy of Sam.

When the service was over, and we left the room I felt someone's hand grip my wrist I turned, my eyes going wide when I saw Oliva looking at me with a small frown on her face.

"Follow me," she said, pulling me along with her. I stumbled a bit, steading my footing as she pulled me over to an empty hallway. She looked left and right, sighing when she confirmed that we really were alone.

"You need to see someone," she said, letting go of my hands before arranging the fabric of her long red skirt. "You need to see a counselor. I'm not sure if you can notice it yourself, but it's getting worse. You're in pain, and you're confused. You need help," she said at a go, making me feel corners. I walked back until my back was pressed against the other wall. I was now across from her, unable to bring my gaze to meet hers.

I hadn't been expecting this conversation. I was tired, and all I wanted to do was head upstairs to my room for a lie-down, and maybe a good cry. Nath and I have been talking infrequently, and that didn't do anything for my low self-esteem regarding how he felt about me. I knew it was because we couldn't meet up like before, but of course, I was worried that he was using it as a way to wean me off him, and I didn't want that at all.

I don't know. I was just nervous like that. The fact that he assumed that I was going to be a coward about things, hurt too. Maybe it hurt even more because he was right.

"Mathew, are you listening to me?" I looked up, realizing that I had zoned out. I shook my head, being honest. Olivia sighed, folding her hands over her small chest. She bit her bottom lip, looking away from me briefly.

"You were shaking up on stage today," she said, and I kept quiet. I didn't know how to reply to that.

"It's getting obvious," she said, turning back to face me. "Sure, they don't know what's obvious, but people will start picking up that something is wrong with you—"

"Something is wrong with you." Her words echoed in my head, and I started heaving. A low groan left my lips as I brought my hands to my face, trying to calm myself down. "Something is wrong with you." Her words continued to echo, bringing me anxiety.

"Olivia," I called out in the middle of her chatter. She had gone on to ramble about finding a good counselor and getting everything fixed. "Oliva," I called out a little bit louder this time, and she finally stopped talking to stare at me with a confused look.

"I'm not going to see a counselor," I said, and she frowned, opening her mouth and then closing it.

"You can't overcome it on your own. You know that, don't you?" she said, moving closer to me. I stepped to the side when she was right in front of me, creating a distance between us.

"You—" I started but sighed. "You won't understand," I finished, resting my back against the wall, and easing downwards until I was sitting on the hallway's embroidery rug. Soon, Oliva was sitting beside me. My vision got blurred as tears gathered in my eyes. I was tired, so tired of trying to come to a consensus in my mind. I couldn't find the right words to use and explain myself to Olivia.

"Come on," she started, letting out a sigh. "If you catch it fast, it won't turn into anything serious. It might feel like the end of the world now..." she trailed. She was right, it did feel like the end of the world, but not for the reasons she thought it did. "But I have your back, and God has your back. I'm sure this is a test, and you're strong enough to overcome it—"

Her words sounded like gibberish to me. They were going through one ear and leaving through the other. I zoned her out, and soon I couldn't see past my blurred vision. I cried in silence as she continued to talk, even though all could hear now was her muffled voice.

I was still spaced out when I felt Oliva's hand on my shoulder. She shook me, making me blink before turning to look at her. She started talking again, and all I could do was give her a forced smile until she stopped and got up from the rug. She bid me farewell, leaving me in the hallway by myself. I sat there for a while, bringing my knees to my chest before resting my head on them.

"Something is wrong with you." A lump formed in my throat as I remembered her words. I shut my eyes, trying to zone it out of my subconsciousness. I stood up soon after, leaving the hallway when I was sure I was no longer crying and was in good enough condition to be seen by others without raising questions.

What do you want? I asked myself in my head as I climbed up the stairs to my floor. Why are you such a coward? I could feel my heart rate increasing again as I beat myself up over it. Making it to my room, I walked in before heading to my bed. My weight sunk the mattress a bit when I sat down. went about taking off my dress shirt, and then my trousers. I was planning to take a nap and try to forget about everything that was going on — it was too overwhelming, but a part of me was restless. A part of me really didn't want to be here saying rehearsed lines and sharing fakes smiles.

My hands were shaking again, and my eyes were blurring with tears as I thought of how odd I had felt up at the pulpit this morning, how out of place and distress I had felt with all the people looking at me. Would they judge me if they knew? Was what had been ringing in my mind. Would they understand if I attempt to explain how I feel?

I was tired of hearing how God was testing me from Olivia and Sam. I was tired of how Oliva and Sam's hearts were in the right place, but they still couldn't understand.

Hiding. I was tired of hiding.

A big part of me wanted to pick up my phone and talk to Nath, but he had retired from trying to discuss anything that had to do with me being gay. I had pushed him away, that was my fault. I was all on my own.

I had to make a choice on my own.

Before I knew it, I was wearing proper jeans and a shirt I just grabbed from the nearest closet. I was stuffing my bag with clothes and other necessities. I was working on automation, knowing that if I didn't do it now I won't have the courage to it ever. With all the haste and hurry to leave the room, I almost left my phone behind. I went back to my study desk, picking it up before scrolling to Nath's contact information.

My finger lingered over the call icon, but I swiped away from the tab. If I called Nath he might try to make me stay back for some reason or the other. Instead, I stuffed my phone in my pocket, walking out of my room before heading down the stairs. I tried to avoid walking into anybody because someone would ask me where I was going, and I wouldn't know what to say. After a painful few minutes of sneaking about and cutting corners because of the voices I was hearing in one hallway or the other, I made it to the main door. I walked out, stunned at myself.

I was out.

A sudden wave of panic took over and I wanted to run back, but I stood still on the spot, willing myself not to turn away. No, I needed to leave.

With the new-found bravery, I continued on my way to Nath's place. I had soon waked far away enough that the station's building wasn't insight. My feet threaded on the dirt road, and my heartbeat filled my ears as I got closer to the street Nath lived on. I knew he wouldn't be home. He had work to do. When I got closer to his flat I say the stray that hung around him run from the backyard before pausing and cocking its head to the side. It had probably been expecting Nath and got me instead.

"Hey," I said to the dog as it whimpered. It shook its tail as I dropped my bag on the floor paneling. "Nath's not back yet," I said, making to sit on the ground before looking out into the street. It was empty as usual. It seemed people minded their business around here. I have never actually seen anything but glimpses of Nath's neighbors. It was early in the evening now, and by my guess probably around five in the evening. I started wondering if anyone had figured out if I was gone yet, and I wondered if Sam would come looking for me.

My lips felt dry, so I licked them before resting the back of my head on the front door of Nath's home. I wanted him to get back soon. I took my phone out of my pocket and was relieved to find out no one had called me yet.

The dog was still walking about the porch, and it came to lay down on the floor beside me. I reached out and pat its head, smiling down at it. "He should be back soon," I said to myself more than I said to the dog. I was a bit nervous about Nath's reaction. I wasn't sure what he would do. He might let me in as I hoped, or he might tell me that I was being ridiculous and that I should go back.

"I love you," I practiced saying out loud. It felt odd on my tongue, and it sounded a bit embarrassing to say. Should I say that to him when he gets here? I felt my lips, frowning a bit before sighing and covering my face with my hands.

"I might freak him out." Distress was beginning to take its toll on me.

"It'll be fine," I whispered to myself as I started to panic again. "Everything will be fine," I tried to convince myself as I waited for Nath to get back. If anything could prove to Nath that I wasn't messing around, this was it. I wanted him, and I had thrown everything away from him. I just hoped he saw how hard of a decision it was for me.

It started to get dark, and I sat by the doorstep, waiting with the dog that had now dozed off.

Chapter Nineteen

"Mathew?" My eyes opened up at the sound of my name. The dog that had been lying beside me got up and started barking and wagging its tail. I squinted, trying to look into the street. There were no street lights here, so it was dark. I could only make out a figure. The person walked up the stairs and was soon on the patio under the orange fluorescent light. It was then my fogged mind realized it was Nathaniel. My eyes went wide, and my heart was beating as I looked up at him.

"What are you doing here?" he asked me, and I just shrugged, bringing my knees to my chest before hugging them. I wasn't sure how much time had passed. I had napped around seven in the evening, and now it was... I looked about, noting how dark it was. Gosh, how long have I been sleeping? I wondered to myself as Nath walked closer to me. He bent over a bit, reaching out to push stray strands of hair away from my face. He was wearing a jumper and a pair of slacks. It let myself watch him massage my cheek with the base of his thumb.

"What happened to you?" his voice was void of shock this time. It was softer. I looked into his dark eyes, wanting to reach out to him so I could latch on to him and cry, but my throat was oddly dry, and I couldn't make a sound. I just looked towards the bag sitting beside me, and Nath's gaze followed mine. I turned to face him. His eyes had an unreadable expression, and he seemed to stiffen.

"You — You left?" he asked, and I just nodded. I watched him bite his bottom lip before letting go of my face. He straightened out, letting out a sigh as he ran a hand through his frizzy hair that he had out today. No buns, not braids, just his hair.

"Gosh—"

"I wanted to leave," I said, cutting him off before he could go on a rant about making decisions on a whim. My gaze followed him, watching as he looked down at me again. I want to be with you Nath. That was what I wanted to say. That was what I should have said, but I muttered something else entirely.

"I was tired of everything. I don't know. I don't want to be there anymore," I groaned, covering my tired eyes with my hands. I felt something wet on my ear. It was probably the dog trying to comfort me.

"I won't ask," Nath said, as I listened for the sound of his feet on the floor. "But I'll help," he said as I felt a hand on my shoulder. I took my hands away from my face, staring at him with a mix of emotions.

"Come on, let's go inside." I wanted to cry — of joy that is. I scrambled up to my feet before adjusting my clothes. Nath had already picked up my red backpack and was looking through his pocket for his home keys. When he found them he opened the door, and I followed him inside. We left the dog behind, making the poor thing whine. Emotions whirled up inside me as I followed him to the kitchen, taking a seat by the counter as I watched him get things from the fridge.

"Do you want anything to eat specifically?" he asked, and I blinked, realizing that I had zoned out. I haven't been in Nath's place in a while. Maybe over a month. Everything was still the same. His hot water kettle was still in the same place I had last seen it, but God it's felt like forever. The past few months with him resounded like a continually pressed piano key in my head. He was all I could think about — all I wanted. I couldn't really think back to when my life was boring and simple. I couldn't really think back to a time when I wasn't thinking of Nath.

My eyes followed him. The smell of his cooking still filled the room. He soon approached the counter with two plates, dropping one in front of me with a fork before giving me a small smile.

"Are you feeling better?"

"Yeah," I answered in a low soft voice, pocking at the vegetables on my plate. "I just couldn't be there anymore."

"I understand," he said, and I smiled a bit, turning to watch him pick at his own food too.

"You can stay here as long as you like." What if I want to be here forever? I wondered, watching him put a forkful of food in his mouth. "You can have the guest room if you want privacy, or you could share my room with me," he let out the second half of his statement like he wasn't sure if it was an appropriate thing to ask. My cheeks flushed, and I looked away.

"I'll stay with you in your room," I said, looking at Nath from the corner of my eyes. His smile widened as he hummed at my response.

When we were done eating I followed him to his room and ended up sitting at the edge of the bed, not knowing what to do.

"You can take a shower," he said, making me look over to him. He was rampaging through his dresser, and soon enough he tossed a clean towel at me. "You can use my stuff. I'm sure you didn't bring much with you," he added, making me nod, as I cradled the towel to my chest. I got up, heading for the small bathroom attached to the room. When the door was closed behind me and it was just me in the small white space I just stood there and let the events of the past few hours was over me.

I was in Nath's house, not my room at the station. I had chosen Nath. My heart was beating fast, and I was a bit overwhelmed. I was happy, and yet I was still confused for some reason. Maybe it was normal. Maybe I just needed time to relax.

"You have to cut yourself some slack. You just ran away from your life for God's sake," I laughed at myself, but it was a dry laugh filled with nervousness, and maybe a hint of self-depreciation. I decided to take my clothes off before approaching the sink to look at myself. I looked like I expected to look, with my eye surrounded by dark circles, and a tired-looking expression. I touched my face, before looking at the shelf for toothpaste and a toothbrush. He said I could use his stuff. I reminded myself as my eyes looked at the products.

They were a lot. I hadn't really thought men used so many products, but what did I know? All the women I talked to didn't use much cosmetics either. On further inspection, I realized most of them had a lot to do with hair care. It did make sense. He did seem to really pay special attention to his hair.

I took a shower, spending extra time to meditate. The sound of water hitting the tiled floor below was relaxing for some reason. Nath. I was at Nath's house, using Nath's shower shampoo and body wash. Nath, not the station. I kept reminding myself. When I was done I dried off my body then wrapped myself in the towel he had given me before walking out into the bedroom. My stomach almost sank from the shock of seeing Nath stark naked and drying his hair with a towel by the edge of the bed. His laughter soon filled the room when he looked my way with a raised brow.

"What?"

I didn't say anything in reply. My eyes were focused on him. I wasn't sure if I should look. I wasn't sure if it was rude, but I just couldn't look away. He really is handsome. A little voice in my head was starting to sow seeds of doubt in my mind. Sure, he was messing around with me, but he could do a lot much better.

"I took a shower in the guest bathroom if that's what you're wondering," he said, walking over to his dresser before pulling out a pair of shorts. "Why are you staring?" he asked, turning to face me again.

"Sorry," I apologized, closing my eyes with my palms on instinct.

"It's no problem." I heard him say. "You can open your eyes, you know. You need to get into something too," he laughed, making me take my hands away from my face. Nath was laying down in bed now, looking at me with a peculiar look on his face.

"Just grab anything from my drawer," he said. I nodded, walking over to it, before pulling it to look inside. It was probably the immature part of me that was shy and flusters by having the man I liked sitting on his bed with only boxers on, and it was probably that same part of me that made me turn red when I realized I was probably going to be climbing into his clothes soon enough. I picked a loose pair of shorts, finding my way into them without dropping my towel. I'm not sure I was ready for him to see me naked. He was really handsome, and I was — I'm not sure how to put it? lean and quite plain.

When I was done changing I hung up the towel beside Nath's on the rack before heading over to the bed. I laid on it, moving under the covers a bit, and my breathing started acting weird. I've been beside Nath on his bed before. It wasn't a big deal.

I don't know.

My mind was still overthinking things when I felt Nath's hands reach out to me. My eyes went wide in surprise when he pulled me closer to him by my waist. I was soon cuddled up to him with my hands nesting between us as he ran a hand through my hair.

"You've been through a lot," he said in a low tone, pulling away from me a bit so that he could look at me. "You're handling this well."

I didn't trust my mouth to say anything, so I didn't. I just nodded, watching as he smiled before leaning in to kiss me on the lips. His lips were soft as usual. A sigh left my lips when he made to pry my lips open with his tongue. I obliged, relaxing into the open mouth kiss. Small sounds kept leaving my lips, but Nath wasn't pulling away and he seemed to even encourage me to make them. I was a little flustered, and my face only got redder when he raised his body and moved to hover over me.

"Wait!" I somewhat squealed, and Nath moved away just as fast, retreating to his side of his bed. I heard him let out a string of curse words after that, and I just stared at the ceiling as my heart raced.

"I'm sorry—"

"You didn't do anything wrong, I'm just..." I trailed, not knowing what to add to that. What was I? I had left the station. I shouldn't be afraid of anything, should I? I wanted to be with Nath in that way, but my mind was just fogged over, and everything was just confusing. "I don't know, I panicked. I'm sorry," I mumbled instead, turning to find Nath staring at me. He sighed, opening his mouth like he wanted to say something before he closed it again.

"Mathew." I looked up at the sound of Nath calling my name. "You don't have to do anything you don't want to do. Don't feel pressured, okay?" I nodded, and he smiled before making to turn away. It's like a little alarm went off in my head at that, and I reached out to him, pulling at his shoulder until he took the initiative to turn back to face me. I didn't give him much time to think because I reached out to cup his face in my hands before moving forward to kiss him again.

Somehow, we got tangled up with each other, he was pulling me closer, molding my body with his and I nested my legs between his. It felt good — great — to be able to touch and see him. I swallowed back my fear when I felt his hands move to touch my chest, my thighs, and then between my legs. His touch was soft, none intruding.

"Push me away if you don't like it," he whispered into my ear as he pressed a kiss to my forehead. He didn't have to worry about that because I was shaking and quivering with the explosion of pleasure in my head. It was a new feeling, something I had thought about, but not experienced before. I wanted him to feel good too, so I mimicked his movements with my own hand. The lack of confidence that had clouded my thoughts before was gone. His vocal encouragement meant the world to me. I was an amateur being an amateur, he had probably had better, but it made me feel happy whenever he moaned into my mouth or told me it felt good when I dared to touch him below his midriff.

We didn't do anything further, but I felt complete and content nested beside him on the bed. We talked for a while, and I told him about what Olivia and Sam had said, and he asked me questions about my family, and about what I wanted to do. He was supportive, none intrusive. He generally backed down from a discussion when he realized I didn't want to have it. Of course, I kept looking at him. I was drinking in his appearance. He was stunning when fully clothed, more so when he wasn't.

When he was asleep I allowed myself to touch his face, his hair, his upper body. I allowed myself to take in his whole being. I leaned close to his ear, muttering the words I love you. I had been too shy, and a bit stunned by everything that had happened this evening to say that to him at the appropriate time. Also, I didn't want to come off as lovesick and desperate. And maybe I was afraid of dragging my two-dimensional idea of what a relationship should be into things.

There was no reaction to my words from his end. Obviously, he was asleep. I closed my eyes, cuddling up to him again under the covers before willing myself to fall asleep as well.

Chapter Twenty

I came to learn that rumors and information spread very fast in the small town. Although everyone seemed to mind their business, something had definitely changed in how I was being treated. The lady at the local convenience store even changed some of the goods I brought to the counter because 'that's not what Nathaniel buys.' People knew I was living with him, and I wasn't sure if that was a good or bad thing. Since I ditched my missionary uniform more people waved at me and even greeted me. I guess from their perspective was no need to avoid me anymore. It's funny how beliefs shape social bubbles.

I wasn't even angry. I kind of understood why they had avoided me then. If I had a chance I would have pulled them aside for a chat like any missionary would, and them deciding they would rather avoid that was not really any different from when church members encourage you to leave the 'difficult people' for people more spiritually strong. There was a huge fear of contamination — not of sickness, but of divergent ideas.

Most of the time when I saw people from my church I would panic and find another route. I wasn't ready to be confronted by them. I knew the drill, they wouldn't offer anything helpful and would just make me more confused and out of touch with myself. Olivia and Sam tried to call many times, but after a week I blocked their numbers, feeling that it was the right thing to do.

"Mathew, are you listening to me?" The sound of Nath's voice brought me out of my thoughts. I apologized, sighing as I rubbed my eyes. He just smiled, picking at his eggs. It was five in the morning, and we were having breakfast in the kitchen. Nath had something to do at the shed, so he had to leave the house earlier than usual.

"I was asking about what you wanted to do," Nath said, picking at his toast. "Were you planning to go to college before?"

I thought about it a bit, realizing that after doing my missionary service I hadn't really had a lot of plans. My father had talked about trade/technical college a few times, and that had been about it.

"If you need a job right away there are a bunch of places that would take you," Nath went on, folding his toast before taking a bite. He chewed, swallowing before he continued. "There are a bunch of stores around here. There's also a library here that's understaffed..." he trailed, pausing before starting right at me.

"Am I being overbearing?" he asked in a concerned tone. I shook my head, rubbing my eyes again. I knew Nath was just trying to help.

"Have you talked to your family since then?" Nath asked me, and I shook my head. I hadn't written home since I left the station. That was about a week plus ago. I guess I was stalling, and I wasn't even sure if they knew now. It was likely that someone took it upon themselves to inform them.

Nath didn't say anything, and he just kept eating his food. I started to pick the boiled eggs on my plate too, but the uncomfortable silence lingered on as we ate.

"I'm just worried," Nath spoke up, making me look over at him. "It's just...
I've been through this and it can be very hard. You're doing amazing," he
said, reaching out for my hand. I looked down at our joined hands. His
dark one, squeezing my pale smaller hand.

"You can't attend church anymore, right? If you want I could drive you out
of town to the Catholic chapel I visit. It's not like anyone will know if you
know what I mean. It's not the same but a church is a church I guess," he
mumbled, rubbing the base of my hand with his thumb.

"It's okay, I'm fine. You don't have to do that," I said, and he just smiled,
taking his hand away from mine. I stared at Nath, thinking about what
he's been through. He acted like leaving his mother didn't faze him and
throwing away a big part of your life like religion was such an easy thing to
do. Or maybe it was, and I just wasn't cut out for it.

"How did it go?" I asked, watching as Nath rose a brow at me.

"Can you tell me how it went—" I paused, licking my lips. I've been putting
off asking him this, but I really wanted to know more about him, and how
he came to most of his conclusions. "With your mum. How it went when
you came out?" I asked, and Nath just stared at me with a blank look.

"You don't have to tell me anything if you don't want to," I added, hoping
that he understood that.

"No, it's okay," he said, dropping his fork. "It's not really one main event,
it's more like a series of events," Nath started.

"So, when I was thirteen she sent me out to a Christian camp. I mean, it's
typical, a Christian mum sending you to a Christian camp." he shrugged
as a small smile formed on his face. "I had fun, it's not like something
extremely terrible happened or anything. We had regular activities, but
there was also the Christian activates if you know what I mean," he said,
and I watched as his face dimmed.

"We used to have bible study every thirty minutes of the day in the morning, and a long one hour talk outside with a preacher in the center, talking about God. You know the usual," he said. "I was Catholic, and there was special attention on none Christian kids in the camp, and kids that were not the 'right' type of Christian, if you know what I mean. It's an evangelical Christian camp, so 'the wrong types of Christians' would be Catholics, etc."

"I didn't really care much, but there was one talk that really hit me. You know, it was a time when people started talking about LGBT+ people. No one was pretending they didn't exist anymore, so of course, they were preaching against them." Nath paused. "I already knew I was gay then. The religion thing was confusing for me because I was trying to meet a compromise."

"The man that was talking to use that day said: 'Imagine if heterosexuality is a clear glass of water, and homosexuality is a glass of water, but with a drop of milk in it. What cup of water do you think God would drink?'," Nath said. "I remember thinking that it was such a shitty thing to say. And I remember thinking God must be shitty too for being so picky about his children," he laughed at his words, sighing before he reached out or his mug of coffee. He brought it to his lips, taking a sip before he set it down.

"It was just such a shitty thing," he sighed, shaking his head.

"On the last day, of course, the counselors would pull us aside and ask us about our home environment, give us some pamphlets and all that gaze..." he trailed. "All I could remember was feeling very angry and confused. I didn't feel bad for being gay, I was angrier that God didn't want me because I was gay if that makes sense," I said.

"If you don't want me, I won't force you to want." Nath shrugged. "I'm not going into a relationship with — in this case, religion, where I have to compromise my personhood to be accepted. That sounds toxic."

"After camp was over, and I went home. I went about my life and all, and I remember not being able to take all this God-talk. I don't know. It felt really patronizing and exhausting. I told my mum I was gay a few years later and she broke down in front of me and told me why I didn't have a dad, and how I was breaking her heart by turning out the way I did. For a few days, we didn't talk. We just stayed in the house together minding our own business. I noticed she didn't go to church that Sunday, and the Sunday after that, and the one after that..." he trailed. "And one day she just dumped a duffle bag in front of my door and told me to leave. She told me I was giving her nightmares, and I should know why."

"So, I left." The room went silent after that. I didn't say anything, and Nathaniel went back to eating his breakfast. When he was done he got up and washed his plate in the sink.

"I'll be back early today," he said, turning back to face me as he dried his hands in a hand towel. "Call me if you need anything."

"Okay," I said as I watched him walk over to me, bending a bit so that he could press a kiss to my forehead. He cupped my face in his hands, peppering my forehead and cheeks with kisses. he pulled away, and I got up, moving closer so that I could hug him. He hummed, causing his chest to vibrate.

"I'm sorry."

"For what?" Nat asked me as we swayed a bit.

I frowned, thinking about it. What was I sorry for? Maybe for pushing religion on him when he had such a bad experience with it? I'm not sure.

"I don't know..." I trailed, shrugging when he pulled away from me. "For bothering you with all the missionary stuff, in the beginning, I guess."

Nath let out a loud laugh, and I watched as he shook his head. "No, don't be. Missionaries have their hearts in the right place, I think most people just forget how triggering it can be for some people."

My lips remained in the thin line as I thought back to home. I remembered a returning missionary talking about approaching random people that looked like they needed prayer to pray with them. Now that I think about it, it might have seemed patronizing and demeaning to the strangers he randomly approached.

"I would love to just hug you and stare at you, but I have to leave," Nath said, and I nodded. His hair was in twists today. I liked it, it looked nice. I followed him out of the kitchen, and out the front door. I stood by the front door and watched as he walked down the stairs and started walking out of sight. I stood by the door until I couldn't see him again.

My eyes moved from the roads to the flat beside us. The lady that was taking out her trash waved at me, and I waved back. I then closed the door and headed for the study where Nath kept most of his books, spending my day reading as I waited for him to get back.

They were interesting to read. Most of them were Catholic-based. I've never really asked why Nath had so many books on faith. Sure, he talked about liking theology, but it seemed more like an off-thought thing — like he was trying to clench on to something.

"The religion thing was confusing for me because I was trying to meet a compromise." I remembered Nath's words from breakfast and I felt conflicted. Compromise? Was there a compromise to be made with Christianity? Nath didn't think to seem there was.

Chapter Twenty-one

Nath was humming as we walk side by side on the path leading to the clearing by the artificial lake. We've been taking strolls like this together in the morning, and there was something special about being able to hold his hand and not worrying about if I had enough time left to stay with him. It was about six in the morning, and he had a few hours until work.

The stray dog was with us today, and it was walking by Nath's side, as usual. It would brush up Nath's pant leg with its body and tail, and occasionally running ahead of us and looking back.

When we got to the clearing we did what we usually did. We just stood and stared at the slow-moving water together. The songbirds around the surrounding trees were loud today, and so were the frogs that were camouflaged on the moss and stones at the edge of the water.

"Have you spoken to your parents?" Nath asked me. I looked up at him, before muttering a small 'no.' I watched him grimace before sighing. He's been worrying about that for a while, and even when I told him it would sort itself out eventually, he was still worried.

"I'll take to them," I said out loud, looking down at the small granite stones by the water. "Eventually," I added. I couldn't even convince myself that I would. It sounded like a badly worded lie to myself even. I wanted to talk to them. Sometimes I went over to read the last email that my mother sent me when I was feeling homesick.

Take care of yourself and reach out to me before anything else.

Her words had been clear, but I was still afraid to talk to her. Any problem she imagined I could have faced was as far away as possible from the possibility of me living with another man. Nath had told me he had been any religious mother's worst nightmare, and I was beginning to feel the same way.

"I'm just asking because I think you need closure," Nath said. "I mean, it's not like I expect them to be understanding. I just think it's better to get it over and done with," he said, and I nodded, feeling him squeeze my hand.

What will my parents say?

They're my parents.

But they're also part of the church.

Are they Christians before my parents, or my parents before Christians?

All the words I had scribbled in my journal just yesterday started to flood my mind. There were a lot of shitty thoughts that involved the possibility of officially being excluded from my family's life. I wouldn't be able to talk to my sisters or parents again. What happens then? Do I just not have a family after that?

"Mathew."

"Sorry," I sighed, running a hand through my dark hair with the fingers of my free hand. I always overthought this. I was worried, really worried.

We stood side by side in silence, not saying anything as time passed. The day began to get brighter, and the baby blue color that bathed the landscape was getting a warm yellow tint as the sun rose above the clouds.

You said you left some stuff in your room back at the station?" Nath said, making me turn to look up at him.

"Yes." That was true. I had packed so fast, and so little. I had left most of my stuff behind. I wondered what they had done with them. Where they were still there, and it would be easy as popping over and getting them.

"Are you going to get them?" Nath asked me, looking down at me. I shrugged, turning my gaze back to the green-blue waters. I wasn't sure if I was ready for the anxiety that would involve.

"I can go and get them for you."

My eyes went wide as I looked up at Nath. His face was blank like he had said a perfectly normal statement.

"It's your stuff. What are they going to say, that you can't have your stuff?" I opened my mouth but looked away when nothing came out. I didn't want Nathaniel to get tangled in my mess, but I guess he already was.

I didn't answer him, and Nath just sighed.

"I'll try and get your stuff later this week," he said, and I didn't protest. I heard the sound of him looking through his pockets. He took his hand away for a bit, and I looked up to find him lighting a cigarette. When he placed it between his lips and took a deep breath he reached out for my hand again, squeezing it gently with his larger one. I squeezed his hand a bit, turning my eyes to watch the waters as the frogs hiding in plain sight croaked. We walked back to his flat a few minutes later. We took a shower together, and I sat at the edge of the bed when we were done. He talked as he moved about the room and got into his clothes, but I wasn't really listening. All my mind could think about was my family back home, and how they would react to the news.

◻◻◻◻◻◻◻◻

To: JiHeePark@gmail.com

Subject: I'm not sure if you're aware of the recent developments.

I'm not sure if the station has reached out to you, or whether Sam or Olivia has messaged you. I'm sorry about not contacting you more recently, but I've been in my head a lot and you could say I've been afraid of your reactions.

If you're reading this and wondering what I'm going on about, then it's probably not reached home so I'll tell you.

I left the station. More like ran away.

I'm in love with a man, and I'm currently living with him.

Why is it so hard to type the word gay? I wondered to myself, sighing as I stared at the email I was typing up. I was in Nath's study with my laptop. It was about seven in the evening, and he just got back from work. Why is it so hard? I wondered again. Why was it so hard for me to call myself gay? Even around Nath. I bit my bottom lip as I went about typing the rest of the message.

I'm not sure how you will receive this (I have an idea, and I'm guessing not very well), but I just want you to know that I'm still Mathew, that nothing has really changed. It was more of a realization than a change.

He's a good person mum.

I wasn't even sure what I was typing up anymore. What was I trying to do? Explaining why they shouldn't write me off as their child?

His name is Nath.

I was talking to him, and I guess it just happened. I don't know.

I continued to write, not really knowing where I was going with the email.

I'm sorry.

I'm sure you'll be disappointed, but I hope you and my father find a place in your hearts to reexamine this. I'm your son, and it would spell out the end of the world for me if you throw me away.

I love you all back home. I really do. Tell my sisters that I love them.

With that, I ended the mail and pressed send. I stared at my computer for a few minutes after that, letting the reality that I had finally reached out to them wash over me. Now I had to wait for their response — or lack of a response. It could be either way. I'm not sure what they would do. I haven't seen my parents angry before. When they were upset they just got really quiet, and maybe my mother would cry a bit. I was sitting at the study desk with a blank stare when the room's door creaked open and Nath walked in. I blinked when I saw a plate of cake get placed in front of me.

"You messaged them?" he asked, sitting on the desk, before looking down at me. He had a piece of cake on a small plate too. The lady at the grocery store also sold nice plain cakes Nath liked to have at home.

"It'll be alright," he said through his bites, and I smiled, picking at the piece of cake on my plate.

Nath talked about every and anything to distract me, and it made me feel warm. I was happy that he was concerned. When we were done with the cake we left the study for the bedroom. I laid down beside Nathaniel, watching him read as I held on to the hand. Just been around him made me less anxious, and it felt great whenever he paused what he was doing to give me a kiss or ask me if I was alright.

We haven't gone all the way yet, but it seemed nice to be eased into everything. You could say things were hotter and more intense about our intimacy, but Nath generally seemed to know when to stop and let me breathe. I was still getting used to it. Of course, I wanted it — all of it, but I was still an inexperienced person that got nervous and overwhelmed.

"Mathew."

"Hmm?" I answered, looking up at Nath.

"Do you want to go out of town again? To the bar... We could head to the Catholic chapel first if you like," he said, and I looked down at his arm, squeezing it a bit as I thought about it. I was no longer afraid of getting caught. Everyone pretty much knew what was going on, and there was a warm feeling that came with realizing that everyone there would know I was with Nath when I got there.

"Sure," I muttered, and I looked up to see his smile reach his eyes.

"Great," he said, leaning in to kiss my forehead before pulling away. I watched him close his eyes, and I held on to his arm as he drifted off to sleep. It was nice to just look at him. Nath looked at peace when he was asleep. Like he wasn't carrying the invisible load he carried in the day. I still wasn't an expert at helping him navigate his feelings. I was personally a walking disaster, and I envied the fact that he could live like his wounds didn't exist.

Chapter Twenty-two

We were in the chapel in the next town. It was quiet, so quiet. All I could hear was Nath's low humming, and he was sitting right beside me with his eyes closed. What was he doing? Was he praying? Meditating? I let my focus rest on the cross at the center stage up front. Yes, I haven't really seen crosses with a crucified Jesus on them, few denominations used it.

The church was a large one with fancy stained-glass paintings. We've been sitting here for the past hour, and how grand the place looked still fazed me.

Nath had brought me here because I asked, but I didn't fail to see that he needed it too. I found myself bending over and holding my clasped hands to myself as I tried to reach into that part of me that believed in prayer. We sat in the chapel until people started to file in and fill the pews. Nath nudged me, whispering in my ear that people were coming in for evening mass, and we should probably leave.

I followed him out into the parking lot, and when we got into the car Nath turned the radio station to a talk show before driving out of the clearing and into the main road.

"Did it help?" he asked after we had been quiet for a while. I looked over at him before muttering a small 'yes.' A smile formed on his face as he made a turn.

"I'm glad," he said, and I smiled too, resting my back on the car seat as I looked out the window to watch the passing scenery. It was six in the evening now, and Nath was taking us to the bar we came to the last time. I still wasn't going to drink alcohol, but I was sure I'd be more willing to loosen up and have fun.

When we got to the clearing Nath packed in it was already past seven in the evening, the sun had gone down, and the evening was dimly lit with the street lamps, and lights coming from the bar itself. I could hear the music when Nath wound down the window glasses before winding them up again and opening the door so that we could get down.

"Come on," he said in a calm voice, startling me. I hadn't noticed that I had just been standing still and not doing anything. "Come on, you'll have fun, I promise," he said with a smile as he reached out to take my hand in his, squeezing it lightly before dragging me to the bar with him.

When Nath pushed the door open and dragged me inside with him, I was hit with hot air, loud music, and the moving dance lights. I wasn't given much time to process everything since Nath pulled me through the crowd of men as quickly as he could until we made it to the front of the bar.

He smiled at me as he helped me get on top of a barstool before sitting across from me. "It'll be fine," he said before looking over the bar to the bartender. "Hey, can you get me a shot?" he asked the man behind the bar. He was a skinny man with a wide smile, and long hair he styled into a ponytail.

"Which one?"

"Anyone," Nath answered, making the man hum before he looked over at me.

"You?"

"I—"

"He'll have a glass of juice," Nath said, answering my question for me. The man behind the bar laughed as he nodded with a hum, fixing up Nath's drink before getting me a glass of juice.

I held the glass in my hand, watching as Nathaniel drank from the small glass he was given.

"What?" he said, making me blink. I muttered a string of apologies when I noticed I had been staring, and he laughed, smiling at me as he held on to his glass of alcohol. "You stare at me a lot," he said, and I felt my face warm up. "It's okay, I like it. I guess I just wonder what's so interesting," he hummed, making me cock my head to the side. His hair was in a low puff today, and his skin looked glowing today. Maybe it was the alcohol, maybe it was the lightning, or maybe it was one of the many face creams he carried around with him.

"Won't you drink your juice?" he asked, making me look down at the glass I was holding with an awkwardly tight grip. I lifted the glass of juice to my lips, taking a sip of the juice — grape.

We sat by the counter, taking a sip as the music changed and people moved around together, dancing, kissing, chatting, and singing along to the loud music. I wasn't sure what I was listening to. It was not the type of music Nath enjoyed, which was more of rap, alternative, and jazz. The songs the bar played were 'bubbly' if that was one way to describe them. It seemed like something people would jump around to with their hands in the air.

"We're happy to have Rachel Tension here with us today. Give her a round of applause, people!" someone said, as the little stage at the far end got flooded with lights, people crowded around, and there was clapping as a woman with big hair walked up on stage and started addressing the crowd.

"A woman?" I said in a partial statement and partial question. Nath laughed, shaking his head as he got off from his stool.

"That's a drag queen," he said before looking over at me. "Are you coming?"

With the nod of my head, I got down from my stool too before following him through the crowds until we were standing close to the stage. I knew what drag queens were, but this one really looked like a woman, she even had breasts and hips, and it was interesting to watch as she sashayed through the stage while lip-syncing to the song that was playing.

"Breast and thigh plates," Nath said, placing his hands on my shoulders before giving them a small squeeze. "She has breasts and tights because of them," he said, answering the question that had been floating in my mind. I wasn't sure how he knew I was curious. Maybe I had been staring at her for too long. My mind seemed to move to the fact that Nath was now pressed up against me and giving my shoulders a massage. The drag queen was still moving about the stage, touching the hands of men and screaming something along the lines of "serving fish!" I couldn't really concentrate on her anymore, and my full attention was now on Nath's hands as I felt them move down to my waist as leaned in and rested his head on my shoulder.

"Relax," he whispered, and I nodded, hoping he couldn't hear how loud my heart was beating because I could hear it in my ears. I closed my eyes. I knew no one was looking, and if they were they didn't really care. I just needed my mine to believe that too.

"Math?"

"Hmm?"

"I love you." Nath's words made my heart beat even faster. I reached for his hands, pulling them away from my waist before turning in his grip.

"You do?" I asked, looking up at him. He looked a bit startled by my reaction, but he soon smiled, nodding before he pulled me to himself.

"A lot. I love you a lot." My heart felt like it was about to burst, and I was so stunned that I couldn't get words out of my mouth, so I just reached out to hold his face in my hands before pulling him down slightly so that our lips could meet. It was a small quick kiss, but it made my face burn. The smirk on Nath's face when I pulled away told me that he was happy with the outcome, so I tried not to beat myself up over the sloppy kiss.

"I love you too," I said in one breath like I was afraid I wouldn't get to say it in the future if I didn't act fast. Nath just hummed, cupping my cheek in his hand as he smiled at me.

There was a round of applause which meant the drag queen was probably done with her performance. Nath squeezed my arm, making me look up at him with a raised brow.

"Do you want to go somewhere private?" he asked, and my cheeks grew warm. He laughed, but I found the will to nod anyway. He pulled me out of the crowd, and we soon got to the main exit. He led me back to the car, opening the doors before hopping into the car. I assumed we were leaving and started to make my way to the other end until Nath reached out to hold my hand and pull me back.

"Come on," he said, tapping his lap like it was the most obvious thing in the world. I stop there with my mouth a bit open for a while. Nath rolled his eye, reaching out and pulling me closer before I got the hint to climb into the car. Somehow, I managed to fit in there with him, facing him as I sat on his lap.

"There," Nath said, as he slammed the door close. He turned to me with a grin before reaching out for my face. It was dark, and I could only make out the outlines of his face, and the twinkle in his eye. The light from the streetlights and the bar that was close by helped a bit. I understood why Nath hadn't turned on the car lights. It would be awkward is someone spotted us out here.

Nath was feeling my face, tracing my lips with his thumb finger as he hummed. My eyes were drooping a bit, he leaned in, giving my lips a ref peck as his hands found their way under my shirt, feeling my chest as he continued to pepper my face with kisses. I was letting out little hums and sighs as I adjusted my position on his lap. I began fiddling with his shirt too, letting my hands roam — palming, and gripping as he moved to kiss me full on the lips.

With red faces and swollen lips, we eventually pulled away from each other. Nath grinned, then he chuckled as he made to brush my now long hair back.

"You're getting better."

"Yeah?" I asked.

"Yeah," he answered with a firm voice as he helped me into the passenger seat.

I was smiling, a wide almost painful smile was spread across my face as Nath started the car and drove out from the clearing and into the main road. He was smiling too, and it made me even happier. The man I was in love with was in love with me, and I wouldn't opt to have it any other way.

The buzzing of my phone in my pocket made me blink. I reached out to get it and looked through my messages before a small sob escaped me.

"What happened?" Nath asked in a concerned voice, but I just shook my head as I held on to my mouth.

Message from: Eomeoni.

You're my son before anything, Mathew.

Your mother loves you.

SAT, 9:48 PM.

My mother's text only made this night better. I calmed down, wiping the happy tears from my eyes before putting my phone away. I looked up to find Nath stealing a glance at me. He looked worried, but his demeanor seemed to change when I smiled.

"My mother texted me," I said, and he let out a small 'oh.'

"She said 'you're my son before anything.' I could cry. What am I saying? I've already cried," I said with a small cheerful laugh. Nath's grin widened, and when he reached out his free hand for mine I gripped it and let him squeeze it. As he drove the rest of the way back to his place, I made a mental note to call my mother later.

I was so happy.

Chapter Twenty-three

Everyone's eyes were on me as I walked into the station. Nath had come along with me, but I had convinced him to wait outside in the car as I went about gathering my things. Hallways would go silent whenever I walked past people, and most of them looked wary, and maybe cold.

When I made it to the room I used to share with Sam I took a deep breath, biting down on my bottom lip before saying a small prayer.

I guess I was nervous. I haven't spoken to Sam in a while. I let myself reach out for the doorknob before turning it and pushing the door open. The room was empty, and Sam was nowhere in sight. I let out the breath I had been holding before walking into the room and heading for my bed. I rose a brow in confusion when I spotted a pamphlet with a book on my bed. I reached for it, and it took a few seconds for me to realize what it was. I tossed it back to the bed in irritation before I went about packing the stuff on my desk, bed drawers, and cupboards.

"A pamphlet suggesting a counselor, great," the irony in my voice could cut through the tense atmosphere in the whole station as I packed. I know the teaching for being gay and Mormon — celibacy, and teachings on how to maintain a heterosexual marriage in the future — I couldn't do what it asked, and I couldn't believe I thought it was such an easy and simple solution before I was the center of concern. That was what was happening with Sam and Olivia. They thought they were helping, but they really weren't. They couldn't understand.

Earlier in the morning, I had talked to my mother. She said she reached out to the station, but they couldn't change their minds on things. I was excommunicated, and I had to deal with that since I was resisting 'help.' Yes, I was free to do as I pleased now, but it stung to know that I was being removed like a nuisance or infection.

"Hey." I turned at the sound of the familiar voice only to see Olivia standing by the door. Her red hair was up in a high bun today, and she was in one of her floral dresses that hung just below her knees. "You're not taking that with you?" she asked, and I followed her eyes to the pamphlet on my bed. I looked away, packing up the items on my bedside table.

"You don't have to do this you know. You just need to agree to get counseling," she said. I looked over at her again, and then away from her. I wasn't in the mood to entertain her words. I went about zipping up the bag I had come with. It was one of Nathaniel's work rucksack. It was now filled with my clothes, books, and other belongings. I was really saying goodbye to this place and in extension all I've ever known.

Getting up from the floor, I lifted the bag before making for the door. Olivia didn't step aside. She stared at me straight in the face. She was about the same height as me.

I looked down at my feet as I let out a sigh. "Please step aside," I asked in a firm voice. I didn't want to fight with Olivia. Or rather, I didn't want to leave here and remember my last encounter with her being a negative one. She was one of the few friends I really talked to, and even though it hurt that she didn't understand, I didn't want to hold it against her.

"You don't have to do this—"

"Move," I said again with a higher firmer tone. Her eyes went wide, but she still didn't step aside. "Please." I think she heard the shaking of my voice with the last word, and with a bit of hesitation, she stepped aside. I was taken aback when I walked out of the room to find people standing around it. I didn't know what they were doing here, but I knew I didn't want to be around them.

"Excuse me," I said, moving past them, and then half walking, half jogging down the stairs to the hallway, and then to the main door.

When I got out my eyes were already teary, and my face was tearstained. I managed to make it to Nath's car without breaking down. He got down, taking the bag from me before placing it in the back seat and heading back to the driver's seat. I got into the car too, rubbing my eyes with the back of my hands as Nath started the car. The station was soon out of sight, and I had calmed down.

"Everything will be alright," Nath said, reaching out to give my thigh a small squeeze when I had finally stopped crying. A small smile took form on my face, and I nodded before resting my head on the car's dashboard.

"Olivia wanted me to stay back," I said, and Nathaniel sighed.

"You'll make new friends," he said, before pausing as if noticing something was wrong with his wording. "What I mean is, you can't always keep the people you want in your life," he said, and I looked away from him as the car continued moving through the roads. It came to a stop soon, and I rose my head to find his flat. The dog that followed Nath around was walking about the front as it usually did. When Nath got down from the car it approached him, barking in delight.

"You might as well adopt it," I said, making Nath shake his head as he closed the door of the driver's seat behind him to get the bag with my belongings.

"Dogs are too much work," he said, closing the back door before we headed into the house. his time he let the dog in, and it half ran, half walked to the warm mat in the living room. Nath disappeared into his room — our room — to drop the bag before he met up with me in the kitchen.

I loved to watch him cook. It wasn't something I had learned at home, so I couldn't really help him out. Sometimes he would ask me to hand him things, and I would.

"How come you can't cook?" Nathaniel ask me as I watched him pour sliced meat into a pot of boiling water. I watched him close the pot before he turned to look at me more evenly.

I sighed before shrugging. "I'm not sure. I guess it's not just something I 'had' to learn if that makes sense."

Nath cocked his head to the side a bit before raising a brow at me. "Something you didn't have to learn? It's basically a life skill," Nath said, and I just stood by the counter with folded hands. I shrugged again, looking away. Why did it feel embracing? I didn't really know any other boys that could cook.

"I'll teach you," I heard Nath's voice say over the silence. I turned to look at him and noticed he had opened the pot again to slice some onions into it.

"Thank you," I said, and he just smiled without turning to look at me.

Since Friday I've spoken to my mum over the phone. She asked me if I was doing alright and told me that my father was still stunned and couldn't talk to me yet. That was fine. I hadn't been expecting him to take easy either. She talked about arranging to see me sometime, and I talked to Jessica over the phone like everything was alright.

I snapped out of my thoughts when I heard the sound of something sizzling, looking over I saw that Nath was setting up the oil for the deep fry. Nath was humming and moving about as he cooked. Thinking about my mother made me want to ask Nathaniel a question.

"Nath."

"Hmm?"

"Have you talked to your mum since you…" I trailed. "Left?" I added, turning to face him. He had dropped the half of the onion he wasn't using on the wooden counter before looking at me.

"No. I don't have her number, and I'm not even sure she lives where we did anymore," Nath said, letting out a sigh. "It's been five years. I know you're worried, but I'm alright. Don't bother about it." Nath had a deep frown on his face now, and his grip on the counter made his dark skin pale in a way that looked dangerous.

"She doesn't want me in her life, and it's fine," he sighed. "I shouldn't have been born anyway."

"Nath, don't say that—"

"Why it's the truth?" he said, frowning at me. I was trying to calm down, but alarm bells were ringing in my mind. Nath was usually calm, and it was odd to see him in so much pain. He wasn't hiding anything today. What I was seeing was raw unfiltered emotion. The yelling had made the dog start barking from the living room. My heart was beating. I didn't like seeing Nath like this. He was in so much pain.

"She's still your mother. She probably didn't think it through—"

"Your mother, isn't my mother, okay?" he said, cutting me off before glaring at me. "I scare my mother. My mother didn't want me. I was her 'cross' on earth as she put it. Do you think it's okay to make someone else miserable just because of how I feel? I don't want to make her miserable."

I wanted to say something to counter that, but I just looked away and bit my lip awkwardly.

The sound of the meat boiling was the only noise in the kitchen now, and I cursed myself for making everything awkward. It might as well be my superpower.

"Sorry," his voice was low now. "I didn't mean to raise my voice," he said, sighing as he brought his hand to his face to massage his temple.

"No, I'm sorry. I brought it up," I muttered, moving closer to him so that I could take his arms in my hands. "I'm sorry," I repeated, giving his hands a little squeeze.

"It's okay," he muttered, and after a while of just staring at him, I let him go. I walked away to the far end of the counter, turning back to stare at him. He looked calm now, but his jaw was set dangerously tight. He went about opening the pot of boiling meat again, and soon enough he was moving about the kitchen and searching the cupboards for ingredients.

Maybe I should just mind my business from now on. I thought to myself as I watched Nath continue cooking. The episode was scary. I wasn't aware that Nath could look that angry — that helpless and defeated.

Chapter Twenty-four

It was around ten in the morning, and I was in a pair of sweatpants and a loose shirt. I smiled as the lady behind the counter helped me check out. Her coworker had gone in to see if they had a brand of corned beef that wasn't on the shelves, and the lady was taking her time to talk to me as we waited.

"How's Nathaniel?" she asked, smiling as she pursed her lips and let out a low whistle. She was a woman with greying hair, and it seemed like her eyesight was failing since she kept squinting at the objects she would pick up and take a look at. "He hasn't been here in a while," she added, dropping the can of peas on the counter before looking straight at me. Her definition of 'in a while' was probably a few days. Nath came here quite often.

The store was empty apart from me, which was typical on a weekday morning since people had gone out to work, and the kids in town were in school.

"He's doing fine," I muttered, resting my hands on the counter as I looked over at the clock hanging on the wall behind her. How long does it take to check a supply room? I wondered.

"Glad to hear," the lady said. "Please take care of him. I've known the boy since he was a twig," she said, emphasizing how skinny he had been by putting her two pointing fingers together. "He'd come here and cry for hours at a time. A woman with children doesn't forget that."

My eyes went wide with sudden investment. I was interested in what she had to say now. Did she know Nath since he was seventeen? I knew he came over to the store quite often, and he seemed to be in better terms with the lady than he was with most people in the town.

"He's a good kid, can't really imagine why his mother would drive him out because of who he is," the lady said, smiling as she leaned in a bit over the counter. "Well, she missed out on meeting the nice boy her son snagged up."

I wasn't really interested in the compliment she was tossing my way. It seemed even though Nath spoke to her, she didn't exactly know why he had been thrown out. Her thinking that it was because he was gay was probably an assumption. I would have made that assumption too. I guess I was the only one that knew what really went on with his mum.

The woman continued talking, but I really wasn't listening to what she was saying. My mind was on Nath, and how I felt kind of hopeless about the whole situation. I could pretend that nothing was wrong, and just let him bottle things up like he had always done, but what would be the point? It would be a recipe for disaster.

After a while, the lady that went in to check if they still had corned beef came back with a can in her hand. I thanked her, and the older lady helped me check out. She slipped some cigarettes into the plastic bag, telling me they were on the house for Nath. I thanked her before I picked the plastic bag with groceries off the counter and left the little store. It was warm outside, and silent since most people had headed out to work or school.

I wondered what Sam and the others would be doing at this time. They were probably having a group prayer and walking from house to house to spread the word. I felt a little queasy at the memory of walking around in the missionary uniform morning after morning in my first few weeks here. Things have changed so much since then.

When I got back to the flat I dropped off the groceries in the kitchen before heading to the study to read. It was something I loved to do now.

Read, read, and read.

I think I understood why Nathaniel loved theology. It was a way of participating in religion from the outside. It did give me less anxiety than prayers. Praying often left me wondering if I was allowed to pray. Asking God for things felt a bit foolish now because I always thought of someone scoffing down at me.

Why would he answer me if I was basically a walking sinner at this point?

□□□□□□□□

"Are you awake?" The sound of Nath's voice made me raise my head. Sometime in the day, I had wandered out of the study to eat, then moved to the bedroom to take a nap. I sat up on the bed, rubbing my eyes with the back of my hands as I heard Nath's movements in the background.

When I opened my eyes and found Nath in just a pair of shorts standing by the window. I wrinkled my nose at the smell of smoke, before bringing my knees to my chest.

"How are you? Were you sleeping all day?" he asked, turning to me, the butt of the cigarette in his hand still burning bright red.

"I'm fine, and no," I answered as he approached me. He put off the cigarette by smashing its butt on the ashtray on the bedside table before sitting next to me. He moved to kiss my cheek, and then my forehead. A small smile formed on my lips before my lips parted to let out a small yawn. How long have I been asleep? I felt numb.

"You were in the study?"

"Yeah."

The room went quiet for a bit as we stared at each other. Nath eventually laid down on the bed, moving his body in a way that he was still able to look up at me with ease. I smiled down at him, letting my fingers run up and down his torso. he had a nice body, and I couldn't help looking at him, and touching him sometimes.

"Mathew."

"Hmm?"

"About that day I yelled at you..." he trailed, moving upwards so that he could reach out and wrap his hands around y torso. "I'm sorry. I guess I haven't gotten over things like I thought I have."

I didn't say anything in response I just reached out and ran a hand through his hair. I wanted to be there for him, but I didn't want to be a pest.

"I was the one that was being nosy. I'm sorry," I muttered. "It's just..." I trailed, turning my gaze over to the window. "You do a lot for me. A lot. I'm in your house, and you do most things. I can't even cook to save my life. The least I can do is try to help you, but it seems I suck at that too."

"It's the least I can do as your boyfriend." I paused, frowning a bit when I realized this was the first time I was saying it out loud. I was his boyfriend, right? We've never actually talked about that before. I bit my bottom lip as I tried to think back to if there was a time we specifically mentioned we were dating or even implied it. Now my stupid brain was busy worrying.

The room had gone silent, and I'm not sure what I was waiting for, but it definitely wasn't Nath's laugh.

"Your face is so red," he chuckled, moving closer so that he could rest his head on my lap. I adjusted a bit so that he wasn't snapping his neck in half to do it before I let my fingers play with his hair twists.

"It's just — I don't know. We've never actually thought about dating, I just assumed—"

"We're dating," Nath said, cutting me off. "Don't worry. I'm just as bad as this romance thing as you are. I've never actually had a proper boyfriend," he confessed as he let his hand move under my shirt. For some reason, his admission made my stomach churn with delight.

"About my mum," Nath started, making me look down at his face again. His eyes had gone a bit dull, and his lips were in a thin line now. "I'll be going back to my hometown for something sooner or later. I guess I might drop by to meet her, but I don't expect anything exceptional to come out of that," he said, and I did my best to undo the crease on his forehead but rubbing it with the base of my thumb.

"I don't have a grudge against her. I just don't want to be a bother," he continued. "I just want to see how she's doing, and if my mind could just stop worrying over the tiny details and making me feel like I'm a terrible person to want to see my mother, that would be great." His voice was shaky now, and I just continued to rub the base of my thumb on his forehead.

"You're not terrible for wanting to see her."

"I wish I could believe that," he sighed before closing his eyes.

I didn't say anything about that. I just let out a sigh as I moved my fingers to play with his hair that was in single twists today. "I could go with you,"

I suggested, and Nath turned a bit so that he was looking up at me with a surprised look on his face.

"Really?"

"Yeah, it's not like I have anything doing," I said, and Nath smiled, muttering a small 'okay' before turning on my lap again so that I had access to his hair.

"About that, are you going to take the job at the library?" he asked.

"Yeah," I answered, remembering that I had been offered a part-time job there. Sorting books? I could do that for sure. The other workers there were nice, and for the most part, the place wasn't crowded. It was mostly old people and school-aged children that came in to use the computer that visited the library. It seemed Nath was a regular there as well since the lady behind the desk immediately noticed him when I walked in with him to talk about the job.

Nath suddenly pulled away from me and sat up. "It's already late. It's around eight in the evening," Nath said. My eyes went wide, and I looked over at the window, noticing how dim it had gotten. I had slept for a long time, hadn't I?

"Do you feel like going to bed? Or do you want to have dinner first?" Nath asked, making me look over at him. I gave it a little thought. I've been asleep for half of the day, so going to bed wasn't the first thing on my mind.

"I don't feel sleepy," I mumbled, and he nodded at my reply before leaning in to peck my nose, then my cheek, then my neck, and then he pulled away.

"Dinner it is then," he said, getting up from the bed before making his way to the room's door. I watched him walk away, and soon the door had shut close behind him. I wasn't sure my chest and face felt warm. Maybe I had been expecting him to do more than peck me? A groan escaped my lips when I noticed that my mind was in the gutter. We hadn't gone all the way yet. I was happy he was trying to ease me into things, but I guess I'm getting a bit impatient.

My lips parted a bit, letting me yawn again before I got up from the bed and left the bedroom for the kitchen as well.

Chapter Twenty-five

"C an we see him?"

"Mum."

My face was bright red as my mother laughed at the other end. We were video chatting, and she was sitting at the dining table. I could hear movements off the screen, and I knew my father was there too. A lump had formed in my throat a while ago, but it was mostly gone now. If he was uncomfortable with talking to me I guess that was okay. I won't hold it against him. I was in the study room of Nath's apartment while Nat was working on a car he had brought home with him from work. It seemed it had to be done asap.

"Well, why can't I see him? I should know who my son is living with," she rationalized, and I just stared at her as the slightest of smiles touched my lips. It was nice to see that she was bubbly and happy. I had been a little afraid she was just acting brave. Her face showed no signs of lost sleep or tears, and I was very happy about that. The last thing I ever wanted to do was cause my mother pain.

"He's out in the backyard working," I said. "He's a mechanic I'm not sure if I've told you before," I added, and she shook her head before humming.

"What about you? What are you doing now?" my mother asked, making my eyes widen a bit. I hadn't been expecting that question.

"I'm working full time at the library here no, until..." I trailed, not knowing what to add. I bit my bottom lip, watching my mother. I hadn't really thought of anything to do after graduating high school. I was supposed to do my missionary service for two years, and now I was suddenly free.

"I don't know," I ended up sighing, telling my mother the truth.

"Have you thought about college?" she asked, and I shook my head.

"Not really." After my words, the conversation fell flat. I could hear Nathaniel working in the backyard. He should be done soon. He's been out there for more than three hours.

"I don't want to put pressure on you, but when you do figure things out please let us know," she said. I smiled a bit. I liked how she kept talking with plural pronouns, but my father was off-screen.

"Are you eating alright? What about your prayers?" she asked, and I hummed before looking straight at her.

"Nathaniel cooks, so don't worry about me starving," I laughed, and she just smiled. "About praying... Well, I don't know. I just feel 'dirty' while doing it if that makes sense?" I said, and she nodded.

"You're still God's child."

An imperfect one. The speck of milk in the glass of water. I said in my head, remembering what Nath had told me about his Christian camp experience. I opted to just smile at my mother's words. We were talking about random things when I heard the door so the study creak open. I paused mid-sentence, turning to find Nath standing at the door.

"Is that him?" my mother said as loud as she could. Maybe she was trying to gain his attention, and if that was what she had wanted she succeeded because he turned over to my computer at the sound of her voice.

"It's him," I said with a small smile before turning over to Nath again. "I'm in a video chat with my mother."

"Oh," he said, turning.

"No, it's alright she wants to see you!" I said, making him pause before turning over to me.

"Yes, I want to see you!" My mum's voice was unnecessarily loud, and it made me laugh a bit to see Nath in such a stunned look on his face. He let go of the doors handle before he walked over to stand by my seat.

"Good evening ma'am," Nath said in his neutral voice. I knew that voice. It was the one he used to talk to random people while creating a distance. He used to talk to me like that before.

"How are you?" my mother asked him, and Nath smiled, pushing back the loose strands of his hair.

"I'm doing fine," he said before looking over at me. "Don't worry, he's doing alright." My cheeks warmed up at that and I could hear my mother laugh. I rose a brow, noticing that I could see a bit of my father now. It was like he was trying to peek and see Nath without getting caught. My smile widened, grateful that he was at least paying attention to the conversation.

When we were done talking to my mother I put my computer to sleep before leaving the study room with Nath. He had let the dog in, and it was the first thing we saw when we walked into the bedroom.

"This dog is practically your child," I said, and Nath laughed as the brown dog hurried over to him, pouncing about until Nath took a sit at the study desk.

"Your mother seems nice," he said, making me smile a bit as I sat down at the edge of the bed. The mattress sunk a bit with my weight, and the room soon went quiet apart from the sound of the dog panting in the corner. Eventually, the dog left the room, and Nath got up to close the door before returning to the study desk.

"Yeah, she's great," I said, moving into the bed more so that I could draw my feet up.

"What that your dad?" My laugh rang through the room at Nath's question. So, he had noticed the man on the side of the screen.

"Yeah," I said with a sigh, biting my bottom lip as I looked at nothing in particular. The room had gradually changed over the last few weeks. My stuff was littered about the place for one thing, and Nath had made some compromises to make me feel comfortable, like shifting the location of his ashtray and adding curtains to the windows.

"Nath, can I ask you something?"

"Sure," he said, making me smile a bit as I looked down at my hands.

"Do you ever feel guilty when you pray?"

"I feel kind of dead — numb really. There's this constant battle in my head of; God doesn't love you, this is stupid', and 'that motherfucker probably doesn't exist'," Nath said, and I looked over at him. His expression was void of any emotions I could read. "I don't know. Maybe I'm messed up because religion has always been a part of my life. Praying's more or less a habit. A habit that makes me feel angry, but more or less it's still a habit," he said.

I opened my mouth, then closed it when I realized I didn't know how to frame what I wanted to say next. A small frown formed on my face as I thought about it, and I decided to try again. "Do you ever feel like praying makes things worse because you're gay? Like, you're going to get punished because you're gay and you dared to pray?" I knew my words sounded stupid, but that has what's been going through my mind for a long time. Nath chuckled, sighing as he turned in his chair in a way that allowed him to look straight at me.

"No, but then again I'm not as religious as you. I don't think I'm a walking sin like you seem to believe you are," Nath said. I opened my mouth to object but closed it when I realized he was right. I did see myself that way know, and it as confusing.

"If I thought I'd get punished for doing something as simple as daring to pray because of who I am I wouldn't visit the church so regularly, or sit down for confession, or..." he trailed. "Receive holy communion when I feel like it," he added before shrugging.

"Isn't that blasphemy against the holy spirit?" I asked, remembering a bit of what I read from the book on Catholicism Nath had in his study.

"My existence is already a blasphemy. I might as well just do something worth going to hell for," he chuckled. His laughed died out almost immediately, and soon the room went silent again. I didn't have anything to say. Nath's self-deprecating jokes broke my heart, but I didn't want to confront him and make him upset.

"Math?"

"Hmm?" I muttered, blinking when I realized I had zoned out.

"Things will sort themselves out," he said, making me smile before letting out a sigh. He got up from his seat before walking over to me. He was in regular joggers and one of his many tank tops. He joined me on the bed, making me lie down as he hovered over me. He smelt clean like he just got out of the shower. He must have gone to the bathroom immediately after working on the car.

"Nath," I called out, getting his attention. I reached out my hands, holding on to his shoulders and pulling him down until he was resting on me. "I know you're trying to be considerate and all, but I think I want to go all the way now," I said, running my hands over his shoulders as he rested his head over mine. "Please?"

"I'm just worried—" he paused, letting out a sigh before rolling over. He was now lying down next to me, his dark eyes staring at my deep brown ones. "I don't want you to get agitated over it. You'll panic, and not because it's your first time," he said, reaching out to brush the strands of hair that had gotten stuck to my forehead.

"I won't get worked up after," I said, reaching out to cup his face before kissing him. We kissed for a bit, and he pulled away from me when I started getting a bit insistent.

"Tell me the truth, do you really believe what you're saying?" he asked. "You already think somethings wrong with you, aren't you scared you'll feel like more of a sinner if you actually went that far?" Nath asked, letting his hand move between us so that he could move his hand under my shirt.

"It's not that I don't want to do it. God do I want to, but—" Nath paused, sighing. "I really don't want to scare you. I don't want to make you feel like you've 'sealed the deal.' If you wake up this morning thinking you want to go back, I don't want you to feel like you have to stay here—"

"I don't want to go back," I said in a firm voice, cutting him off. Nath's eyes widened a bit, and I think he saw that I was taking offense to what he was saying. Sure, I was still a little confused, and I was still navigating my sense of self in connection with my religion, but I didn't want to leave him. Why would he think that?

After a while, Nath looked away, but he was still touching my abdomen. I felt it heat up, and my toes curl when his hand moved lover. He smiled at that, pressing against me as his lips found mine. When things got a bit heated he became a little hesitant, but I held on to him, showing him that I wasn't afraid at all and I wanted it.

I had him. He had me, and I'm not sure if I could explain the whirlwind of emotions that came with connecting with him in such a way. If this was sin, I wanted nothing else but it. I'll take whatever bitterness that comes with it.

Chapter Twenty-six

"You look surprised." I turned at the sound of Nath's laughter. He was driving us through the neighborhood he used to live in, and the place was a bit shocking to me. Some people stared at us, or rather at Nath as the car drive by. We had picked up some car parts from the repair shop he had intended to visit, and now we were heading for his childhood home. The neighborhood wasn't what I expected it to be. It looked more rural, with flats dotting the landscape — a lot like the farming city I was from, but these people didn't keep gardens or farm animals.

After a while of driving, Nath pulled the car to a stop in front of a flat. He took in a deep breath, and I turned to look at him before reaching out to squeeze his thigh.

"Your mother lives here?" I asked, and he bit down on his bottom lip.

"I suppose. This was where I last interacted with her." I hummed to myself, looking at the house. It was a small one coated with green paint. The garden looked like it hadn't been touched in years, and I didn't see any signs of someone being inside. It didn't look like someone lived there.

"Are you sure she still lives here?" I asked, and Nath just looked on at the house.

"One way to find out," he said, unlocking the doors before coming out from the car. I came down too, following him to the front door. Nath took a deep breath and just stared at the door, it was only when I reached out for his hand and gave it a squeeze that he let out a sigh and made to knock on the door with his free hand. He knocked once, twice, three times, and at the fourth time, I was starting to think that no one was home, or that no one lived there at all.

I could see that Nath was about to give up, but both our eyes went wide when he heard a noise at the other end.

"Who's there?" A voice said from the other end as we heard footsteps from the other end. "I'm asking who's there? Is it the mailman?" The obvious female voice was higher now, and Nath squeezed my hand. He was shaking, and it seemed like he didn't want to talk.

"Ma..." he trailed off, and the questions from the other end just paused. It went silent, and I wasn't too sure what was going on or if his mother was going to open the door.

"Nathaniel?" her voice was quiet now, almost like a whisper. I looked up at Nath, watching him rub his eyes with the back of his hand.

"Y-yes," he stuttered like a little kid, and the front door clicked open. I turned to look over at the woman who was standing at the door now. She was small, around 4'8. Her eyes were wide with shock, and her dark skin paled when her eyes met with Nathaniel's. The two stared at each other for a good minute. Nath's mother looked away first, and her gaze quickly moved to our joined hands.

I couldn't really read the expression on her face, it was masked with so many others that I wasn't sure what to think. She but her lip, looking away from our joined hands back to Nathaniel.

"Is this who you're with?" she asked in her soft voice and Nath just nodded. He hadn't had much to say since she opened the door.

After a period of silence, she spoke up. "He looks like a nice person," she said, and it was then Nath looked her in the eyes again. They were wide, and a small smile and made their way to his full lips. Nath had told me that he was the carbon copy of his father, and while he didn't look much like his mother the smile they both had on their faces looked similar.

"Would you two like to come in?" she asked, and Nath nodded, and so did I. She stepped aside, letting both of us in. I looked about the place as we made our way through the small hallway before making our way to the living room. It looked like what Nath had described to me on our way here, plain and decorated with religious ornaments of all sorts. I was familiar with some of the pictures hanging around, but my church didn't have statues about the place.

"Take a seat. I'll go get you two something to drink," she said, leaving us behind in the living room before walking out to the main hallway. The sounds of her footsteps soon faded away, and I went ahead to sit down beside Nath on the long sofa.

"I thought you said she wasn't religious anymore?" I asked, turning to him. Nath's eyes were scanning the room.

"I thought she wasn't," he said, fiddling with the rosary on his chest. He was dressed differently today. He was in black slacks and a dress shirt.

Soon after his mother came out with a tray of with a juice box and three glasses on it. She placed it on the center table before pouring each of use a cup.

"How have you been?" she asked after a while of all of us staying silent. "I've been worried, and I didn't know where you went or where to start looking," she said, gazing at Nath. She was sitting across from us with her feet crossed, and her hands gripping to the tumbler glass filled with orange juice in her hands.

"I just hoped that you'd come back one day, and sometimes I started wondering whether you ever would, or if you were even in this world anymore." Her shoulders slumped, and she let out a loud sigh before taking a sip from her glass.

"I said and did a lot of things. I'm not blaming it on my break down, but I was overwhelmed and felt I had been cheated out of my reward from God," she said, and Nath just looked straight at her, not saying anything. "'Why would you make my son gay?' 'Why would you torment me like this?' Those were the types of words going through my head then, and I felt faint, scared, and most of all cheated," she added before sighing again.

"Since you left I've had time to think and reflect. I was treating you as a penance for what happened, and when you didn't turn out like the perfect testament I wanted I got angry," she said, and Nathan looked down at his feet, unable to meet his mother's eyes.

"But you're not any of that, you're just my son." Her voice was shaky now. "You're not my medal for overcoming trauma, you're my son," she repeated, and she started to tear up. She dropped her glass on the coffee table beside the sofa she was sitting up. Nath got up and headed over to her, kneeling by her chair before giving her a hug. I felt like a foreigner just staring at them, so I looked down at my feet until they pulled away from each other and Nath stood up.

His mother smiled at me as Nath made to sit beside me.

"I did a lot of soul searching for the past few years, and eventually found myself in church again. I've been praying for you to come back ever since. I've missed you so much, and I'm sorry for treating you the way that I did," she said. "You're the fruit of my womb."

"You're not an extension of my life, you're your own person," she said. "So, I shouldn't have reacted like the food I made went bad."

I watched Nath cringe a bit, but he didn't say anything in response to that. I'm sure he was happy about the sentiment, but the mention of church — any mention of church got him like that.

"Well, how are you?" she asked, turning to face me instead. I felt a bit flustered by the sudden attention.

"I'm fine," I answered as I felt Nath's hand take mine before giving it a squeeze. Squeezing it a bit. We talked to his mum for the next few hours. It was nice to watch them catch up, and I did tell her about myself from time to time. We left her flat with her number and a couple of homemade pastries. When we were in the car I noticed how quiet Nath was being.

"Nath?" I called out, and he looked at me from the side of his eye before turning back to face the road.

"Thanks' Mathew," he said as we made a turn. "If you hadn't convinced me to reach out to her I might have just come over to this town, get the car parts and left."

A smile formed on my face as I hummed. Nath had turned on the radio went we got in so soft alternative music was playing.

"I'm glad things turned out as they did," I muttered, looking down at the box of pastries that he had given me. "She doesn't hate you," I added. If anything, the woman was happy to see him.

"Yeah." Nath's voice was a bit choked, but it sounded overwhelmed with happiness, not sad and woeful. I turned, spotting the smile on his lips as he hummed along to the music in the car. I smiled too. I was glad things worked out.

"She said she went back to church," I said in a low tone. Nath looked at me from the corners of his eyes before shrugging.

"I guess religion is a way for some people to find themselves. Everyone's different. Different strokes for different folks," he muttered, and I hummed in agreement.

Chapter Twenty-seven

"Mathew... Hey! Wait up!" Olivia's voice rang through the street as I continued walking. I thought she'd sigh and go on her way like she often did, but I heard footsteps behind me and I realized she was following me.

"Mathew!" she yelled again. Her voice was closer, and I tried to quicken my pace which is hard to do when you have hands weighed down with grocery bags. I let out a groan of frustration when I felt her claps her hand on my shoulder. I stopped in my tracks, just standing there as both of us let out heavy breaths.

"Mathew," she said again, but with a softer voice. "Didn't you hear me? I wanted to talk to you," she said. My mind felt fogged. I didn't have anything to say to her, and I didn't want to speak to her if all she had to say was 'come back.' I shrugged her hand off my shoulder, and she let out a surprised sigh.

"Why are you acting like this?" she asked as I started walking away again. "What's up with you? Talk to me Math." I paused in my tracks, letting out a deep sigh. It was early in the morning, meaning the streets were empty and it was just her and me on the road. Biting down on my bottom lip I decided to turn to face her. Her face was red from running, and her red brows were knitted in a tight frown.

"I don't have anything to say, Olivia," I said after a while of us just staring at each other. "And if all you have to say are words convincing me that I can change, I don't want to hear them," I continued. Olivia opened her mouth but closed it before letting out a sigh. She folded her hands over her small chest as her lips formed a tight line.

"Friends are supposed to tell you the truth, Mathew," she started, walking closer to me until she was standing right in front of me. "If I turn a blind eye to what's happening, won't that make me a bad friend?" she asked, and I just stared at her. At a point, I would have agreed with her, but now that I was in the receiving end of the almost aggressive concern I wasn't sure what to think.

"Have you ever considered that you might not understand what I'm going through?" I asked her as I dropped the plastic bag of groceries on the dirt road. My hands were hurting from holding them. "You're making me anxious and irritated—"

"That's the spirit telling you what you're doing is wrong," she said, cutting me off.

I rolled my eyes, bringing my hand to my temple. "You don't understand Olivia. Being at the station and having you all bombard me with reasons why how I feel is wrong makes me feel anxious and unwanted. Being with Nath makes me happy. If you were me in this situation wouldn't you pick staying with Nath? Doesn't that seem like an easy enough decision?" I asked, and Olivia just stared at me.

"Sin is sweet — bittersweet. It dresses itself to look attractive, and when you're in its clutches it pulls you into the depths of sorrow," Olivia said, making me groan again. I wanted to leave, but right now I was irritated and had something to say.

"Olivia, I want to ask you something, if that's okay," I said, and I watched as she shrugged.

"Go ahead," she said before using her hands to arrange the material of her floral skirt.

"How come when Christians suffer it's God trying to strengthen us, and when nonbelievers suffer it's God punishing them?" I asked, and she just stared at me. "How come when nonbelievers have a good life or feel happy with themselves it's sin dressing up to deceive them, but when Christians prosper it's God blessing us?"

"You're a lovely smart woman that at one point I called my friend — you're still my friend. How is it that those clear and obvious double standards exist, and we just accept them as fact? Do you really believe people we deem as unbelievers have no chance at happiness? Do you think I'll be forever damned it I choose Nath and not the church?" I stayed quiet after my little monologue and Oliva just stood there. After a while of waiting for her to speak, I sighed, bending a bit to pick up the plastic bags I had dropped when I realized I wasn't going to get an answer.

"See you later Olivia," I said, turning my back to her.

"I'll pray for you." I heard her voice say. I winced at how firm and final it was. It felt like a knife, stabbing away at my back that I had turned to her.

"Prayer's not a weapon Olivia," I said. "Prayer should be done with love, not malic," I finished before I continued walking. I didn't hear footsteps behind me, which meant she probably just stood there and watched me leave.

I was still breathing heavily when I got home. Nath had left for work, so it was just me in the flat. I went to our room, kneeling by the bed as I tried to calm myself down. I didn't want to be angry with Olivia. I really didn't want to resent the people that I grew up and shared memories with. She was just applying what she thought was right in my situation.

□□□□□□□□

"It's annoying," I said before biting into the piece of cake in my hand. I was sitting between Nathaniel's legs on our bed, ranting to him about my encounter with Olivia on the street.

"Well, you said it yourself, she doesn't know any better." I opened my mouth to reply to Nath after swallowing, but I closed it, biting down on my bottom lip as my eyes moved about the room. It was around eight in the evening now, Nath had gotten back an hour ago. I had started working short four-hour shifts in the library, so I still got back home before him even though I left after him.

"I'm not saying you're wrong. I'm just saying it is what it is," Nathaniel sigh, stroking my arm before giving it a little squeeze. "It's okay to be irritated but remind yourself that you only know better because you're on the receiving end."

A sigh left my lips, and I nodded before resting back on his chest. He was right. Maybe I should take out some time and message Olivia and Sam. I had blocked their numbers a long time ago. I wanted to still be friends with them. I really did, but it would be hard with both of them breathing down my throat about my decision. I looked up at him, and he smiled before reaching for my cheek to dust of the crumbs.

"To change the conversation—" Nath paused, bending a bit so that he could give my lips a peck. The peck turned into a kiss, and the kiss into a brief make-out season. When he eventually pulled away my cheeks were warm, and his full lips were slightly red.

"That was a nice distraction," I said, and he chuckled as he pushed some stray strands of hair out of my forehead.

"It was, but that wasn't what I wanted to do." He smiled down at me before looking up at the clock that hung over the bedroom door. "You said your mother was coming over. When exactly?" he asked, and I sat up before bending to the side to grab another piece of cake from the plate sitting on the bedside table.

"In a few weeks," I answered before taking a bit of the piece of cake in my hand.

"I should get the guest room ready them. How long will she be staying?" Nath asked me as he reached out for my hand. I struggled a bit, but we both laughed when he pulled my arm towards his face so that he could take a bite of the piece of cake in my hand. My face was hurting from smiling, it just felt great to be around Nath.

"I don't know how long she'll be staying, maybe I'll ask her about that later," I said, and Nathaniel just hummed.

My mum has been calling us more frequently since I gave her the number to the landline. Nath also had her number, and she had his number as well, but they had never called each other. It was okay — baby steps were okay.

Speaking of baby steps my father was now appearing in the video calls. He would say 'hello' and 'bye', and sometimes he would even input to the discussions I had with my mother. I talked to my sisters now, but even though no one said it I kind of knew I wasn't allowed to tell them what was going on. It was nice to talk to them though. Learning about their classes, friends, and church activities made me smile. They knew who Nath was, they just called him 'uncle.' They knew he was out of place. Jessica had asked about his tattoos, and sometimes ask why I was suddenly allowed to call home. She also asked where Olivia and Sam were, but I had overall gotten better at lying, and it didn't make me feel bad because I wasn't ready to explain my complicated situation to her.

"I like this," Nath said, and I blinked, realizing that I had zoned out. I bit down on my bottom lip when I realized he was talking about us being together.

"I like this too," I said. "A lot."

I really do, I sighed, shifting a bit so that I could look at him properly. We were both in joggers and tank tops. You could say Nath was influencing my choice of clothes now. I didn't mind at all.

Nath smiled as I turned around so that I was facing him. He bent a bit, reaching out for my face before cupping it and giving me a kiss. It didn't take long until I was laying on my back and he was hovering over me giving my face kisses as he ran his hands over my body.

I remembered Olivia telling me I couldn't be happy without the church, but here I was, as happy as ever.

Chapter Twenty-eight

"Mathew." I turned at the sound of a familiar female voice. I looked away when I saw Olivia standing behind me, and she sighed as I went about rearranging the books. The library was pretty empty at this time since most people were at work or school. I kept arranging the books. I even took out some books to place them right back as I waited for Olivia to leave, but I never heard her walking away. The library was decently sized, not huge, but large enough that I was stuck in the middle with Olivia in the midst of towering wooden shelves while the other employees were a good distance away.

I was a bit upset by that. If someone was close I would at least have been able to pretend I was called.

"Mathew, I'm not leaving. You have to talk to me," she said, and I just continued rearranging the books. I heard her sigh again, but this time she walked forward, standing right beside me so that I couldn't ignore her. The small smile she gave me when I looked at her from the corner of my eyes made me almost drop the book in my hand. I reacted quickly and looked away, pretending that she wasn't there.

"Math," she said, reaching out to hold the book I was about to place back on the shelve. "Who do you think you're fooling?"

I opened my mouth to say something, but I closed it and shook my head instead. I left the book with Olivia, and it tumbled to the ground since she hadn't expected me to let go.

"Olivia, we can't have a conversation if you're going to keep pushing the same remedies," I emphasized the last part as I took some steps back. My words made her frown a bit. The worst part about this situation is that Olivia hasn't changed at all. She didn't hate me. she's just trying to help me like she would any member of our church, but it's extremely tiring to try and explain to her why

"I want us to be friends, but I have a feeling you'll keep trying to sneak in counseling as an option. I don't want that. I'm not sick. I'm fine," I said, watching as her lips trembled a bit.

"You're not." Her reply was expected. I felt my shoulders sag, and I covered my face with my palm as I decided to play along and not argue that fact with her.

"You can't cure homosexuality with counseling — with anything," I said. My wording was making my stomach churn with acid. Trying to argue out my attraction to Nath like it was a disease made me frustrated, but I wasn't sure how else to talk to Olivia.

"Why not?" she asked. Her red hair was pinned back in a tight neat bun, and her brows were now in a firm frown.

"It's not going to help—"

"Who told you that? The man you're living with?" she asked, and I stayed quiet. Nath had told me about a couple of his friends that had tried to get rid of their gayness — of course it never really worked, but the horror stories were hard to listen to. I wasn't sure what exactly my church did about being gay, but I did know they pushed counseling for a 'normal life.'

"Yes, he did," I eventually said. I was keeping my voice as low as possible. The other people that worked in the library were all the way on the other side by the main desk, but if they found out Olivia was here bothering me they would probably toss her out.

"And you'll just believe him?" Oliva asked, stretching out her hand before groaning. "Look, the thing about sin is that people never want to wallow in it along. 'Misery likes company.' do you remember that saying? I'm sure you do," she rambled on, and I just stared at her.

"I don't want your help. If you can't respect that, we can't be friends," I said firmly, and Olivia's eyes went wide as if she had just realized what it entailed.

"You don't want to do this—"

"Why not? What else am I supposed to do when you can't just respect my choice?" I asked, and she stared at me with an open mouth. After a while, she shook her head.

"Look, Mathew, I'd be a terrible friend if I just let you walk into an open fire—"

"This isn't fire, Olivia. Can you stop with the terrible comparations?" I asked.

"Mathew, is something the matter?" The voice of the other librarian caught us both of guard.

"No, nothing," I said, watching as Olivia turned towards the direction of the voice before looking back at me.

"If you want to talk with me unblock my number and give me a call today. I'm afraid I'll make a scene. I think seeing you in person is making it a bit too personal," she said in a soft voice, giving me one last look before she turned and walked away. I watched her as her footsteps echoed through the library. I left out a breath when she was out of sight before rubbing the middle of my brows. I was exhausted. I turned away, looking back at the bookshelves to continue what I had been doing before she came up to me.

□□□□□□□□

"Call them if you want to," Nathaniel said, making me look up from my phone screen to stare at him. He was changing out of his work clothes to a comfortable pair of pants and a tank top. "You've been looking at your phone for the past hour," he added, combing his hair with his fingers before walking over to the bed we shared. He sat down at the edge, making the bed sink a little bit with his weight.

I sighed, turning the phone in my hand. I had unblocked Oliva and Samuel a while ago, but I was still hesitant about giving them both a call.

"Do you think it would make a difference?" I wasn't really talking to Nath, but he hummed, making me look up at him.

"The thing is," he started, reaching out to run his fingers through my hair. "If you don't call them and try to sort things out you'll spend the rest of your life wondering what if," he said, making me bite my bottom lip before looking down at my phone again.

"So, you're saying even if things don't get sorted out now, I'll have peace of mind just knowing I tried?"

"Mhm," Nath said before taking his hand away from my hair. I turned to look at him again, and this time he leaned forward to peck my life. We smiled at each other, and we both chuckled when Nath rubbed his nose against mine.

"Call them," he said as he pulled away. I watched as he got up from the bed before walking over to the room's door. He paused, turning to smile at me. My heart was racing. I hadn't quite gotten used to his full-face smile. "I'll be in the living room," he said before opening the door and walking out. I looked on at the door even after Nathaniel closed it behind him. A sigh left my lips as I looked down at my phone again.

After a while of just sitting down and sighing, I went ahead to make a three-way call with Olivia and Sam. Olivia picked almost immediately, and Sam's end rang for a while more before he eventually picked up. We all stayed silent until Olivia spoke up.

"Well?" she asked, making me cover my eyes as I tried to arrange what I wanted to say. It took a while, and when I was ready I wasn't sure if they were on the line with me anymore.

"Olivia?"

"Yes."

"Sam?" It took a few seconds, but he replied to me. I hummed, playing with my fingers now. I had put the call on speaker now, and my phone was sitting on the bed.

"We're not going to agree about..." I trailed, not know what to say. Agree about what really? My gayness? That sounded wrong to say in my head like I was agreeing it was a choice I made when it wasn't. "We're not going to agree with me distancing myself away from the church," I said instead, and I could hear Olivia suck in her breath. Sam's end of the line was dead silent.

"I'm still Christian. I just — I just understand things differently now. I'm still finding my feet, and I want this to be between me and my spirituality, not me and what the church thinks I'm supposed to do," I went on. When none of them but in I continued. "I still want to be friends with you two, but I would love it if you stopped trying to change my mind about something I've made up."

I stopped talking, and there was no other noise in the room but the sound of the fan turning. I could hear some T.V. sounds. Nath was probably watching something in the living room.

"You drive me away with the aggressive intruding. If you want to help me, try praying for me in private. If you push me away, you won't have a chance to help me. Let's not let this ruin our friendship, please?" I begged, waiting for someone to say something. Anything at all. I was starting to panic, but I relaxed when Sam spoke up.

"Fine Mathew," he said, and I let out a sigh of relief.

"Okay." Olivia's voice was small like she felt defeated.

"I'll keep you in my prayers," Sam said, and I just chuckled. The more I spent with Nath, the sillier that line sounded. I was less angry at it and more prone to push it aside as Sam not knowing any better.

"There's a lot of things to be angry at. Ignorance might be one of them but there are just stuff you learn to overlook for your own sanity." Nath had told me one day as he worked on a car he brought home in the backyard. Being upset that Olivia and Sam didn't understand had been my default settings for the past few weeks, but if I thought about it, I would have been touting the same things Olivia had at me if I had never been put on the spot to rethink my positions.

"I'll do that too," Olivia said. We all spoke about mundane things, distancing the religion talk that seemed to always be at the brim of the bucket. Nothing spilled over, though, and we ended the call on a good note. I was smiling when I left the room and headed for the living room. Nath was slouched on the sofa with a bowl of ice-cream. A smile spread across my face. Just knowing I got to be with him made me happy.

"I went well?" Nath asked, watching me walk over to him. I nodded with a hum, sitting beside him before turning my eyes to the T.V. He was watching some weird cooking show.

"That's great," he said, and I just smiled, reaching out to squeeze his arm. Everything was falling into place, and I couldn't be happier.

Chapter Twenty-nine

"If your church won't let you participate, you could just look for one in the next town to pop into every now and again," Nath said, working with screws and some spare parts on the small kitchen island. I shrugged at his suggestion, sighing before I rested my head on the cool surface of the dining table in front of me. It was late noon on a weekday. Nath and I were hanging out. Well, I think you could call it that. I was reading one of the many books from his library, and he was kind enough to bring his work inside with him so that we could see each other. There was something about just being in each other's presence that made me happy.

For the past week, I've been trying to look for a way to still take part in the church. The thing is, I'm not allowed to if I don't agree to meet with a counselor. At this point, there was no difference between me and a none believer. If people knew what — who — I was if I decided to go to a temple, I probably wouldn't be let in.

I closed my eyes at the 'what' part of my thought process. I'm trying my best to get rid of the internalized shit I've been fed for most of my life. If I had to be with Nath, I had to be out and proud. Nath joking about closet cases and insecure gay people being annoying was just a joke, but it hit home for me, maybe a little too hard.

The sound of Nath drumming on the kitchen island with the plastic end of his screw made me force my mind to go back to the discussion at hand—attending church.

"It's not because you're gay," Sam had said to me the other day when I pulled him aside to ask about not being able to attend service or Sunday classes. He had been in his missionary uniform that day. I saw that he had a new partner that day and looked kind of worried to be seen around with me. I had pushed his behavior aside, pressing him on about it.

"Then what is it?" I asked, raising my voice a bit. His partner had coughed, probably trying to signal to Sam that he wanted to leave.

"It's because..." he never finished that sentence, he just bit down on his bottom lip before looking down at the ground. "Look, why are you asking me this? I'm working now, can't you talk to another elder or the counselor?"

Counselor. That word made me nervous, and I hadn't been sure if Sam had been acting in good fate. My mouth opened, but I didn't say anything, so I just looked away and sighed before leaving him to walk back to the library for my shift that morning.

It was annoying because I couldn't even attend service with them even though missionaries brought in people they were talking to all the time. What was the difference between me and them? Before I actively started to inquire about this, I thought I could shoehorn myself into the church while keeping my distance. Despite my decision to practice Christianity from my understanding and not in accordance with the doctrines of a specific church, growing up Mormon was all I knew, and of course, most of my understanding of what Christianity was from being Mormon.

"Mathew?" I blinked, realizing that I had spaced out again. I let out a sigh, sitting up and covering my face with my hands before sighing.

"It's okay," Nath said with a small smile.

"It's just..." I started, trailing off when I wasn't sure what to say. "I don't know. I'm not sure about another church," I said, biting my bottom lip. Nath gave me a small smile before getting out of his seat and heading to stand behind me.

"I'll follow you into the next town a few times to go to church, so don't worry about that." He was running a hand through my hair now, and the mix of him touching me and speaking to me softly calmed me down.

I leaned back a bit so that I was resting my head on his midsection. We stayed like that for a bit, not saying anything.

Nath let out a small hum as he let go of my hair and headed back to the kitchen island to continue working with the spare parts.

"In a few days your mum will be here," he said, making me smile as I nodded. I've been counting down the days to the day my mum said she would get here. I couldn't wait to see her -- I couldn't wait for her to see Nath.

"What?" I asked, noticing that Nathaniel had gone a bit quiet. "Is my mum coming going to be a problem?" I asked, starting to feel a bit nervous. I had just realized that although I had told Nath about her coming, I hadn't really asked him if she could come.

"No," he said in a firm tone shaking his head in a way that made his twists bounce with the action. "I'm just nervous, that's all," he laughed, and I raised a brow at him, leaning to the side so that I could look at him properly.

"Nervous?" I asked, not sure what to say to that.

"Yeah," he replied with a smile, dropping the screwdriver he had in his hand. "Nervous... You know? That thing you are when you're not sure what will happen," he said, and I rolled my eyes before leaning back on the wooden seat.

"Why?" I asked, and Nath shrugged.

"Maybe she won't like me," he said before looking around the small kitchen. "Maybe she won't like this house, who knows," he said waving his hands before looking back at his tools. I rested my head on my hands watching him with a look of interest plastered on my face.

"She's going to like you. She already likes you even," I said, making Nath hum as he cleared the kitchen island of his tools. He was packing up and would probably lave for the bedroom in a while. Nath had a very strict pattern of doing things but watching him follow his routine over and over again never got boring.

"Yeah, nervousness isn't always rational," he said, taking down the small tool books from the surface before walking past me and out of the kitchen. After giving it some thought, I got up from my seat at the dining table before walking out of the kitchen as well. I noticed that Nath had gone into the bedroom we now shared. A sigh left my lips as I followed him in, wondering what he was up to. Was he going to take a nap or have a smoke? Somehow, I've managed in his place without caving into taking a cigarette, alcohol, or coffee, but then again, it wasn't like Nath was trying to get me to try them. Of course, he thought some of my beliefs were silly, sometimes he was outright rude about them (which is something he was trying to change) but he never pressed me over mundane things.

"What?" he asked, after turning and noticing me at the door. I shrugged my shoulders, not saying anything. I just liked being around him, and maybe this wasn't the time for that since he seemed agitated by our small discussion in the kitchen.

He rolled his eyes at my response before taking off his shirt and jeans so that he was only in his boxers. He then climbed into the bed. It sank with his weight, and he shifted a bit until he was rested against the pillow he propped up.

"Are you still worried about my mother coming?" I asked from the front door, breaking the silence.

Nath stayed silent. He opened his mouth, then he closed it before folding his hands. "I'm sure you think it's ridiculous, but I just want her to like me. I don't know..." he said as I walked over to the bed, before taking a seat on the edge and looking out into the room. The place was getting a lot more crowded with my belongings, and it made me happy. I just felt at home here. It was my home.

"Don't want to be the person that led her son astray," Nath whispered, making my eyes go wide as I turned to face him. I reached out to give his shoulder a light shove. He was laughing now, and I was laughing too, and although we were joking about it there was a sinking feeling in my gut because I knew people went through that. It was a privilege to joke about it.

"Really though," he muttered, making me look over at him again. His smile was reaching his eyes, and I loved the way he was looking at me. He leaned in a bit, pecking my lips, and I pulled him back for a full-on kiss when he made to pull away from me. We kissed for a bit, and when we pulled away I was red-faced and he was grinning.

"I like that you're initiating stuff more," he said.

"Me too." He raised a brow at my reply, and I just shrugged, picking up the book I had been reading in the kitchen from the bedside table. I liked that Nath was trying to give me space to think about my faith, but the same way I only knew about Mormonism at a personal level, he only knew about Catholicism at a personal level. I've been reading a lot about his childhood faith, but it was — different. There's no other way to describe how different the two denominations were.

"Have you spoken to Olivia recently?" Nath asked, making me shrug. Yeah, we talk when we bump into each other from time to time, but apart from the random small talk and light smiles, we didn't talk all that much. Samuel outright avoided me unless I went up to him. The fact that I was slowly losing my friends was a bit heartbreaking. After all the effort I put in. I thought to myself as a sad frown made its way to my face.

Nath sighed, leaning on me. "You don't have to keep friends, you know? People move apart, it happens. And you know, you're trying, so if that happens you know you've tried." I felt the tip of his thumb rub against my palm. It was calming.

"I guess," I answered taking my hand away from him. I pulled my legs up from the carpet so that I was sitting with my legs folded on the bed.

"And you'll make new ones," Nath said to me, raising his head from my shoulder. "I have a lot of friends. You've even met some of them."

I laughed, shaking my head. Nath's friends were... something. Also, it felt a lot being introduced as his boyfriend to the people he used to sleep around with. Nath rose a brow at my laughter, but he just smiled, reaching out to hold my hand.

"Suit yourself," he said in a teasing tone. My smile just widened as I looked down at him. He had somehow snuggled his head into my lap. I reached out to turn his twists between my fingers. I liked this. I liked being with him, and I hoped my mum was just as enthusiastic about him when she got here as well. My mum liked good people. Nath was a good person, and maybe she'll see past the awkward clothing and tattoos unlike me when I had first looked at him through the bus window.

Chapter Thirty

"He's very tall," my mother said as Nath left us behind to bring the car closer to the entrance. I found myself chuckling before I rolled my eyes. Of course, his height is what she would have noticed first. It was late in the afternoon on a Saturday morning. My mother had arrived at the tiny town a few minutes ago. She had taken the bus, and that was why we were currently standing outside the bus station as we waited for Nath. I was wearing casual clothes, a pair of jeans and a long-sleeved top I had to roll up because they were Nath's and were too big for me. My mum was in her regular long skirt and loose-fitting blouse look.

I had been nervous to meet her after the past couple of months, but she had been bubbly and happy like she always was, so I calmed down and became more open chatty as well. She was going on about the renovations to the kitchen back home, and how she was excited to be finally getting a dishwasher. It made me smile. She really was a simple woman.

"So, what have you been doing for the past few months?" she asked, breaking the silence that had washed over us after her last sentence. I shrugged, leaning off the pillar I had been resting on before looking out into the parking lot. There were other people here as well, but it was mostly empty.

"I've taken up some hobbies..." I trailed, taking my eyes to the ground. "I got a job, I learned to cook—"

"You can cook now?" she asked, making me look up at her. She sounded surprised and curious. I smiled, nodding before looking away.

"Yeah, Nath taught me," I said, taking out my hands from my pockets before playing with my fingers. My skin was tougher now, and I was more tanned thanks to taking walks with Nath and helping him out with more physical things.

"He can cook?"

"He lives alone, he would die if he didn't know how," I laughed, and my mother just homed. The little farming town I had grown up in was very traditional, and from what I've been learning since I got here, maybe too traditional. I didn't really know many 'girl' skills, and I hadn't been expected to. Now that I think about it, I didn't know many 'boy' skills either. Nath had recently started showing me how to drive, and he was letting me near his tools as well — they seemed foreign, and I still had to ask him how to use stuff time and again.

Nath's car soon parked right in front of the bus station entrance. I picked up my mum's box and she followed me. I opened the back door, and as she climbed in I went to drop the boxes at the back. When I went to sit up front I realized how tense the atmosphere was. Nath started to drive, and none of said anything until my mother spoke up.

"You're very tall," my mother said, making me chuckle. Nath seemed taken aback. He couldn't turn back to look at her, but I could see he was trying to look at her from the driving mirror.

"Well, yes," he said with a small chuckle. Turned to look at my mother, she had a small smile on her face, and she was probably wondering what to say now. She didn't have to say anything since I butt into the conversation, so it wouldn't die.

"How was your drive here?"

"Long," she said, making me laugh.

Soon we were both chatting with my mother about mundane things like the church choir, and how expensive a loaf of bread was back home. Nath was nervous. I could tell from the way his hands gripped the steering wheel. I thought about it for a while before I reached out to squeeze his tie. He turned to me with wide eyes but looked away when I gave him an assuring smile. I think my mother noticed this because she went quiet, but I noticed she was smiling at us from the side of my eyes.

After about fifteen minutes we were at Nath's place. Nath had taken the time to fix up around the house, the place was covered in a new coat of paint — a nice sea green. We helped my mum with her bags, talking to her as she looked about the small street. The neighbors that rarely made an appearance were looking at us through their window. I waved when I caught them, and they waved back. They were all odd like that, somewhat like Nath. There was no shame in being curious here.

The brown stray dog that followed Nath around the place was looking at my mother with perked eyes. I wondered what it was thinking. It probably wondered what the small person with greyish hair was doing here. It walked up to us, and my mum smiled at the dog, bending over to pat its head while Nath laughed.

We took my mum's bags up to the guest room, and Nath left both of us in the room alone saying that he needed to prepare for dinner. The room went silent once he closed the door behind him. It was just me and my mother, and I'm sure she had something to say to me. I turned to her, taking slow steps in no particular direction before I settled on sitting on top of the room's dresser.

"He seems like a nice person."

"Yeah," I said. I was surprised at my own voice. It sounded choked and worried. "Sorry. I just—" I sighed, covering my face with my hand. I wasn't sure why I was crying now, but I was. My mother got up from the bed before walking over to me. She placed her hand on my shoulder, resting against me as she held on to me.

"It's okay," she whispered, and I just nodded, trying to clean my eyes with the back of my hands. My body was shaking, but I was relieved, all the tension from worrying this morning had been washed away. When I had calmed down my mother started to talk about things to distract me. She was telling me funny stories about my sisters and dad. She talked about getting a small vegetable patch, and she asked me if it would be okay for her to cook something for us tomorrow. Soon I was smiling again. Nath's voice soon rang through the small flat asking us to come out for dinner.

Nath had made some sauce and boiled potatoes. The dog was inside too and was hanging around the dining table as Nath and I talked to my mother. It was mid-evening now, and the room was lit by the orange light above us as the day got darker. We talked about mundane things, and Nath seemed relaxed by my mother.

"When did you those?" she asked, pointing at the tattoo on Nath's wrists. He had worn a long sleeve top today despite it being warm to hide them, but one could still see the ones around his collarbone and wrists.

Nath shrugged. "I have friends that are tattoo artists. You go to visit, and before you know it you're getting inked," he said with a small chuckle and my mum looked on at him with a partly confused smile. I wasn't sure if it was because she didn't know what being inked meant, or because she hadn't really seen people with tattoos before.

"Is there anything you want to do while you're here?" Nath asked, changing the conversation. My mum looked down at her plate of food as she hummed.

"I just wanted to see Mathew," she said with a smile before looking up and turning her gaze to me. "Do you still go for service?" she asked, I caught the hint of hope in her tone, and she looked sad when I shook my head.

Great, things are awkward again. I thought.

"He doesn't go to the Mormon church here, but sometimes we go to a Catholic chapel in the next town," Nath said, making me blink. I had zoned out without realizing it. My mum was looking at Nath now.

"You're Catholic?"

"Used to be," Nath said with a shrug before giving the dog that was sitting beside his seat a piece of meat.

"Anyway, if you want to take a walk in the morning you can head out with Math and me tomorrow. The library here's also huge, and they have a nice farmer's market at the end of every week," Nath said, changing the conversation. At the mention of a farmer's market, my mother started asking questions, and just like that, I was left alone to think. I turned to Nath, smiling in silent thanks.

When we were done with dinner. I helped Nath out with washing the dishes while my mother watched us with a curious gaze. She kept asking me how my prayers were going, and how the last few months down here have been. At first, Nath tensed up, but he relaxed when he realized it was my mum just being my mum without any malic in her tone.

"How's dad?" I asked, turning to face her when I dried the last plate in the sink.

"Your dad's fine," she said with a small smile. "He wants to speak with you, so if you can manage it you should call him," she said, and I nodded. The fact that I was nervous yet happy didn't quite show on my face since my expression was void and numb. My dad wanted to talk to me? I was giddy and happy. I haven't spoken directly to him in a long time.

"Nath seems like a great person," my mother had told me when Nat left the kitchen briefly to give the brown stray a treat.

I smiled at her before settling down on the seat across from her. "Yeah, he is," I replied.

Nath was great, he really was. I had a long way to go with accepting myself and navigating my faith, while Nath had a long way to go unpacking the things that happened with him in the past while mending his relationship with his mother. I was glad someone was patient enough with me to try and understand, and I was happy to help Nath out with sorting out his feelings. We didn't always agree, but it worked. We had each other to nurse and kiss each other's wounds.

I couldn't be more grateful.

THE END

www.ingramcontent.com/pod-product-compliance
Lightning Source LLC
Chambersburg PA
CBHW070352200726
48294CB00003B/875